HINTERLAND

BY THE SAME AUTHOR

War and Photography

Hinterland

A Novel

Caroline Brothers

B L O O M S B U R Y

NEW YORK · BERLIN · LONDON · SYDNEY

Published by Bloomsbury USA, New York

All papers used by Bloomsbury USA are natural, recyclable products made from wood grown in well-managed forests. The manufacturing processes conform to the environmental regulations of the country of origin.

LIBRARY OF CONGRESS CATALOGING-IN-PUBLICATION DATA

Brothers, Caroline.
Hinterland : a novel / Caroline Brothers.— 1st U.S. ed.
p.cm.
ISBN 978-1-60819-678-4
1. Brothers—Fiction. 2. Homeless boys—Fiction. 3. Afghans—Foreign countries—
Fiction.
I. Title.
PR9619.4.B758H56 2012
823'.92—dc22
2011020290

First U.S. Edition 2012

1 3 5 7 9 10 8 6 4 2

Typeset by Hewer Text UK Ltd, Edinburgh
Printed in the U.S.A. by Quad/Graphics, Fairfield, Pennyslvania

For Navid, Bashir, Hamid, Alixe, Jawed, Jawad, Ramin, Ramzi, Nazibullah, Rahim, Mushtaba, Ali, Mohammed, Hussein, Sohrab, Reza and Qasim.

'When you start on the way to Ithaca,
Wish that the way be long'

C. P. Cavafy

'How should I make a life?'

Jawad, 14

In invisible squadrons they arrive by night, feather-damaged, pectorals and sinews aching from constant striving into the coastal headwinds. Something otherworldly reels them in to precisely the right place. The little tunnels in the cliff face are still there from the year before, the faded white flags of guano still staking out their entrances in the crumbling loam. Some of the burrows are caving in where the roots of spinifex grass have failed to hold the ceilings intact. Still there, nevertheless, despite the wind and sea-damp and erosion — the shelters where they themselves had hatched, and where their offspring too would huddle before that one long swoon off the cliff-top, all life rushing in on winds that come screeching over the sea and smash into the overland air currents, all faith all consideration all thought displaced by that one most terrifying of instincts: that first blind leap into flight.

It was no secret, and yet it was one of nature's secrets merely because, for eons, it had not been pieced together by man; the long pilgrimage south over abacus island chains, the vast blue meniscus of sea, the ragged coasts of continents unscrolling below like a map, and eventually, arrival, of sorts: staggering on spindle legs, tattered wings flapping once, twice, before folding like pale umbrellas. Theirs was the graceful recovery of *dignity on an island at the southernmost tip of the world. Then, the forlorn muster of those who had made the distance, the others lost somewhere along the highways of ocean and wind and sky. The mating, the laying, the hatching, the fishing, the feeding. And finally, with the ancient earth tilting on its axis, the long journey north, offspring abandoned to the same instinct of navigation that had thrust them and their parents and their parents' parents into one long relay of survival that was predicated upon one overriding task: beating out those nautical miles under the magnetic pull of the sun.*

They have arrived two weeks too late and the river is in flood.

The snows in the distant Balkans have melted early, swelling the rivulets and the mountain streams that feed the wide border river with its annual harvest of silt. The rising waters nuzzle the tree-trunks and steal into the rice paddies that stretch across no-man's-land, turning the fields into opalescent reproductions of sky. Even during the day there are no birds, nor any stirring of life.

Aryan pushes his dripping hair out of his eyes. Beyond the bridge he can just make out the naked trees and in the distance, the steep rise of the far bank that leads to the motorway in Europe.

'Follow me,' says the boy with the withered arm.

The men fall into line, fifteen of them, stumbling through the waterlogged land. They stick to the small ridges between the fields, hopping between islands of grass and earth. Aryan can feel the water seeping into his train-ers, into socks slowly corrugating under the soles of his feet. His shoes suck and slide with every step; he winces at the sound his fraught mind amplifies for miles across the gloomy landscape. Ahead of him, his friend curses his blisters under his breath; between them, Kabir makes big strides on stocky legs, weaving in an extra skip so as not to fall behind.

The hanging clouds which have left so small a ledge between earth and sky mean that tonight, at least, there is no danger of any moon.

Once they halt abruptly. They can see the torches of the border guards blinking and bobbing like fireflies along the narrow bridge. Aryan hopes the soldiers will be unobservant this night; the crossing will end in ambush if the boy's people are on the take from both sides.

Word of mouth – the cumulative wisdom that travels the same routes as men in flight over rugged lands – has warned him about the Turkish jails where those caught in the borderlands rot away their lives. Crouching in the drizzle and the mud, he prays that he has not been wrong to trust this misshapen boy.

But it is not the lights on the bridge that have made their guide so suddenly freeze and drop to his knees. His ears have picked up the sound long before Aryan makes out the grey shadow nosing along the road they have just crossed: an army vehicle, lights out, en route to the military buildings clustered round the bridgehead.

They wait, hunched over but exposed in the open field, scarcely daring to breathe. Aryan can feel the water that has soaked the bottom of his jeans creeping above his knees; there is no give in the fabric where it sticks to his legs, and the wind against it turns his skin to ice. His teeth chatter loud as a sewing machine inside his skull. The warmth leaches out of his muscles, and tiredness weighs like a bad dream.

Finally the boy stands up. The vehicle on its lone mission has disappeared; the soldiers in its fuggy warmth have not seen or not wanted to see the bedraggled creatures cowering against the dark. Unfolding aching limbs the band resumes its march, leaving the sinister hulk of the bridgehead far behind.

It seems as if they have been walking for hours. Aryan keeps his eye on the treeline on the far side of the fields, and notices the water level rising as they approach. He can't hear the river but he can smell it before they reach it, the odour of mud and decomposition and the chill breath of water layering the damp night air. He rolls up his saturated trousers.

In the dimness, the boy slips out of sight and then suddenly reappears, deft as a heron, shoving an inflatable skiff with a long pole. From inside it he produces a heap of sagging rubber and an air pump that the men take turns to use.

The Evros is wider here but the current is still strong. Aryan has never seen so daunting a river – nothing like the waterways at home that dried out in the summer but turned into ravenous torrents in the spring. He tries to gauge the distance, wonders if they shouldn't find a narrower place upstream.

Suddenly he starts; something catches his eye. Kabir

sees it too. A cadaver drifts towards them, revolving slowly in the black water, stiff arms scratching at the sky; the tightness in his chest stays with him even after it morphs into a tree-trunk that has been dislodged far upriver by the rains. He tries not to think of it as an omen, or that others may be following behind to capsize their flimsy craft.

'It's just a funny old log, Kabir,' he says.

His brother grips his hand. His face is a pale disk in the crepuscular light.

Now, at least, they are out of sight of the bridge.

High up on the far embankment the trees judder in the sweep of headlights as the semi-trailers take the curve. Aryan wonders if their truck is already waiting on the other side.

'This is where I leave you,' the boy says. He wears a Turkish evil eye symbol on a leather cord around his neck and rarely meets their gaze. With his one dextrous hand he lights a cigarette and the molten tip of it burns a hole in the icy air.

'Make for that tall tree – can you see it? – just before the river bends,' the boy says in halting English. Aryan thinks they must be almost the same age. He follows the boy's finger; he can just make out the skeleton of an oak in the residue of light.

'When you get there, cut the boat like this.' He makes slashing movements with a pocket-knife in the air. 'Turn it over and sink it. Then if they find you, they can't send you back.

'After that, you climb the embankment to the road. When you get to the wall, keep low. Wait till you hear the truck stop. You must not speak. Come out only when the driver gives the word.'

With his good hand, the boy undoes the rope that ties the first to the second boat and ushers them aboard.

'How long till the truck comes by?' somebody asks.

The boy shrugs. 'Just wait till it comes,' he says. His features are gaunt in the darkness that settles on their skin like ash. 'I go now. Remember, if you get caught, you've never seen me. If you get sent back, we'll take you across again.'

He turns and walks away, a thin crescent that quickly merges with the treeline, leaving only the faint smell of tobacco tracing arabesques over the sodden land.

They push off, skimming across shallows that shiver and pucker in the breeze. There is a hush over the world. Aryan can see Kabir's profile in the darkness, unruly hair flattened for once by the rain. Opposite, his friend Hamid sits in silence, knees pulled up to his chest. No one speaks, knowledgeable of how the open water can betray them. They have come too far now to jeopardize a crossing as dangerous as their separate odysseys through the deserts and mountain passes of Afghanistan, Kurdistan and Iran.

As the river deepens they feel the current accelerate, the pole sinking into the velvety silt. One of the stronger men works it with both hands; the skiff wobbles as he heaves and pulls. Aryan doubts any of them can swim. He looks back without nostalgia at the land they are leaving behind, and watches the second boat push off from shore.

The current lifts them and takes them rapidly now. Through his feet Aryan can feel its power, like something immense and alive, pushing upwards beneath the boat's rubbery floor. Already it is taking water and losing air. Soon the man raises the pole; he can no longer feel the bottom, and stands helpless as they glide rudderless downstream. Landfall is slipping away from them; they are going to overshoot. With frightened eyes the men watch the boatman try to keep his balance, striving to find a purchase as the current snatches at his pole. Finally it meets resistance, and with one mighty shove he propels them towards the shallows. The embankment casts a black shadow over the water as they come aground, well below the tree the boy has indicated, on a stony lip of beach.

The other boat struggles, and comes in above them. The men splash into thigh-deep eddies, cursing and losing their footing and clasping at branches that reach out over the river to haul them in.

Aryan watches as the last man on the second boat lifts it and slashes it with his knife. But it is slippery and heavy with water and slithers out of his hands like an eel, and the current spirits it away.

'I'd love it if the guards were out fishing and hooked that big jellyfish up,' Hamid says.

They stab their dinghy too. The rubber hisses as the air rushes out; it subsides into a limp black membrane. Still they cannot sink it, so they dispatch it after the other one, out into the racing stream.

Battling the undergrowth, they make their way a few yards upriver, and begin to climb through the aqueous night. Aryan's hair sticks to his forehead. Bracken scratches his hands and water runs down the back of his neck. Low branches tear at his anorak, snag on the clothing of the man in front and whip into his face. He hears Kabir puffing and tries to slow his pace to match his brother's, to stop fear speeding his own ascent. Hamid stumbles once and swears. Someone behind them growls at him to keep his voice down.

There is no path, but Aryan tries to still his nerves by thinking of those who must have taken this route before them, imagines he sees the markings of their feet in the clay.

On the highway above them the trucks whizz by, pepper-spraying gravel. Silhouetted branches claw at shifting cones of light. He prays no border police are patrolling the road tonight.

Presently, just as the boy has said, they reach a low wall. They insert themselves into the narrow gap between it and the rain-lashed vegetation, and wait.

Aryan concentrates on his breathing as Omar has taught him, stilling the accelerated pounding of his heart. Someone struggles to smother a cough. His empty stomach complains. He tries to muffle it before the sound of it echoes and reverberates down the valley, loud enough to wake the sleeping houses, rouse the border guards, alert the watchdogs and the farmhands and the truck drivers smoking on the leeward side of their semi-trailers, betraying to the world the presence of fifteen men huddled on a lonely bend in a highway between two worlds.

His mind leaps back to the map he looked up on the Internet, the line of red hatching that was the border wriggling down from the mountains, through the landmine zone, skirting the length of the river to the sea. After that, their journey becomes an illegible tangle of possibilities, of railway lines, shipping routes and roads.

'How long do we wait here?' Hamid says.

Aryan shrugs. 'Dunno, Birdsnest,' he says, plucking a curled-up leaf from Hamid's fringe.

Hamid shakes the debris from his hair. 'They better not have forgotten to send the truck.'

'They'll come,' Aryan says. 'It's bad for business if they let us down.'

'I'm glad you've got such faith in them.'

Kabir leans back against Aryan.

'You're a good soldier,' Aryan says to him. 'Just make sure you don't fall asleep.'

Kabir grins up at him through shut lids. 'Just resting my eyes,' he says.

'Good thing he's not our lookout,' says Hamid.

'I'm wide awake even though my eyes are closed,' says Kabir.

'Well don't forget to open them when the truck comes,'

says Hamid. 'We're not coming back for anyone who's slept in.'

Aryan squirms, pretending to shrug Kabir off. 'Remind me where we're going, Soldierboy.'

'We're going to school.'

'Where?'

'To school!'

'And when are we going to get there?'

'At half past nine!'

'When?'

'On time!'

'And *how* are we going to get there?'

'KabulTehranIstanbulAthensRomeParisLondon!' says Kabir.

'Bravo,' Aryan says. 'But I bet you I'll get there first.'

Hamid grins at Aryan through the drizzle. He has heard it before, the way Aryan has taught his brother to recite the names of the capitals like stepping stones across the map of the sentient world, a songline of seen and imagined places that points to where they're going and where they've been and gives them a hold on the memory of who they are.

Aryan would never tell Kabir that the ritual for him is more than banter; he would never admit to him how much it is inspired by fear. Sometimes he wakes in panic, dreaming his little brother is being swept away from him in a crowd. Sometimes they are separated by smugglers or by uniformed men. Sometimes it's a checkpoint, sometimes a truck stop – each time, he is forced to abandon his brother on the road. If anything happens, Aryan thinks, Kabir will still stand a chance if he can remember where to go, if the names of the cities become coordinates he can navigate by, like the sailors who once set their journeys by the stars.

They fall silent, listening to the dripping trees and the rubber kiss of tyres on the asphalt.

'What's the first thing you're going to do when we get to Europe?' Hamid says after a while.

Aryan ponders. 'Eat the biggest lamb kebab you've ever seen,' he says. 'Then sleep in a proper bed, and get a new card for my phone.'

'That's three things, you fool. In that case I want a giant kebab too, plus a steaming hot shower, and to see Bruce Willis on a big screen. And after that I'll borrow your phone.'

'Sure, then you can pay for the card,' Aryan says.

'True friend,' Hamid says, pinging a pebble at his foot.

'Who's Bruce Willis?' says Kabir.

'Bruce Willis is one big Afghan hero,' Hamid says. 'I saw him in a TV store in Istanbul – twenty of him, all at once, right up to the ceiling – one mighty action man.'

'Bruce to the power of twenty,' Aryan says, surprising himself with the memory of a long-ago class in maths.

'Maybe they'll have *Titanic* too, and films from Bollywood,' Kabir says. He has dislodged a rock from the soil, checking to see whether the centipedes and mudeyes and larvae here are the same.

'What do you know about Bollywood?' says Hamid.

'Lots,' says Kabir. 'There were guys selling DVDs on the street in Iran.'

'Can't you boys shut up?' The voice comes from further down the wall.

'Who's listening?' Hamid shoots back. 'Or do the trucks in Greece have ears?'

Aryan catches Hamid's eye and pulls a face, willing his friend's anger to dissipate. Since they met in Istanbul, Hamid has always been like that, able to reduce grown men to laughter but also quick to take offence, and volatile around authority he cannot charm.

Hamid mutters under his breath, but holds his tongue.

Aryan rests his forehead against the rough concrete wall. He can see crystals of sand like sugar in the cement, the cracks almost wide enough to hide something, to slip a message inside. He traces the jagged line with his fingertip. The adrenalin of the crossing is ebbing now, replaced by an overwhelming desire for sleep. To stay awake, he tries to conjure up the faces of everyone he played football with on Omar's team.

Now that they've stopped moving, his body is starting to chill. His clothes seem to soak up the ambient dampness of the night. He starts to shiver again.

After what seems like hours they hear a semi-trailer slowing as it takes the bend, its wheels crunching on gravel. It growls to a halt. No one dares breathe. Maybe it's not their truck; maybe it's just a driver who has stopped to piss.

Aryan feels a desperate urge to shift; anything to ease the cramp in his legs. Suddenly, he hears a low whistle.

He peers over the barrier. The truck's tail lights glow bloodshot on either side of its number plate. Exhaust swirls like illuminated breath.

'Let's go!' someone says.

One of the men vaults over the wall and swings open the doors. One by one they leap up and dive inside. The wheels are taller than Kabir; Hamid hauls him up by the armpits. Aryan nearly lands on top of them. Seconds later the dark square of sky is obliterated; the bolts of the door squeal as they are locked in. They are still arranging themselves on the boxes in the blackness when the engine engages, the wheels grind, and the vehicle lurches on to the highway. They throw their hands out and grab at whatever they can catch to steady themselves.

Someone coaxes a flame from a cigarette lighter. Weird and distorted against the shadows, their faces are tight as masks.

'Welcome to Europa,' somebody says.

The driver cranks down through the gears until the truck slows to a stop. Voices. Footsteps. The low growl of a dog. The men freeze.

Aryan doesn't know how long they have been driving, or where they are. He reaches for Kabir, finds his shoulder in the dark, and grips it.

The doors of the truck swing open and the night air

rushes in. Torchlight rakes the inside. Aryan ducks and shrinks into the boxes but knows he is not concealed. He can't see who is wielding the beam of light – soldier, border guard, customs officer, trucker, police. It sweeps the rafters, probes the piles of cartons, then locks on him. He can hear his blood thudding in his ears. The light considers him a long moment, bleaching the world white behind tight-clenched eyes. Anxiety fingers his spine. He wonders whether they are going to let the dog loose inside.

'ForgiveMeForgiveMeForgiveMe,' he says to himself, the simplest prayer he ever learned.

After a moment the doors slam shut. Blindfolded again by the darkness, his eyes open to sliding diamonds of red and black.

There is a brisk exchange with the driver, and the vehicle drags itself back on to the road.

They are on their way.

Aryan loses all sense of time. In the closeness of the truck's belly none of them has any idea how far they have travelled, whether it is day or night, what country they are in. In the hours that pass the dimensions of the world are reduced to the sound of the road: the stickiness of wheels on bitumen, the wind-rush of passing vehicles. The men doze, stretch the pins and needles from their legs, fit their bodies to the angles of box and wall. The truck's metal rib feels like a stake running the length of Aryan's back.

Once, the truck pulls over and the driver descends.

Tension ripples through the darkness. Above the thrum of the idling engine comes the rustle of a man relieving himself by the roadside. The endless journey resumes.

Kabir is unconscious, his head warm and heavy on Aryan's thigh. Aryan strokes his brother's still-damp hair. It is getting cold and he pulls the hood of his anorak over his ears. The corner of a box is digging into his side but if he moves he will wake the sleeping boy. He shifts anyway, and Kabir stirs.

'It's OK,' Aryan says to him. The boy's steady breathing resumes.

In the dark he can hear someone snoring gently, and smiles. There is nowhere Hamid cannot sleep.

Aryan's body is tired but his mind won't let him rest. His body rocks with the movement of the lorry. He listens to it swallowing up the miles as it carries them deep into the backcountry, far from the borderland. He tries to remember how many trucks they have been on since they left Afghanistan: sheep trucks, fruit trucks, once, the fume-filled bins of a fertilizer truck – each reeking of dung or decay or chemicals that took days to get out of his hair. Some of the men talk softly.

'Do you know where they are going to leave us?' Aryan can't pair the face with the anxious voice.

'Somewhere outside Patras, I would say.' The rasp of a smoker.

'The problem there is the police,' a third voice says. 'If they catch us they'll send us back across the river.'

'We should break up into smaller groups, just twos and threes.'

'The thing is to find the sea and follow it to the port,' the smoker says.

'It will all depend on where they dump us,' says another voice.

Their urgent whisperings are sucked away in the tunnel of highway wind.

After a while the truck slows. It leans into a long curve, and the men and boxes slide with the motion.

'Why are we leaving the highway?' someone says.

'Maybe it's a detour.'

'Maybe it's another checkpoint.'

'Maybe they're gonna let us out for a piss.'

'Only in first class, my friend.'

The next road is less well made. There is a different rhythm under the tyres, a regular double bump as the wheels hit the joints in the surface. The change in tone wakes men who have learned to listen in their sleep; from the crinkle of their clothes and their silence Aryan can tell they are alert and straining for clues.

'I'm hungry,' Kabir says.

Aryan pats his chest pocket and pulls out a wad of silver paper. He hands Kabir a pillow of Turkish chewing gum. He will feel ravenous afterwards, but the explosion of sugar, and the illusion of food, will trick his stomach for a while.

Aryan folds the last piece back into his anorak, nursing

his own hunger like a secret. To distract himself, he makes a mental inventory of his pockets.

* One brown vinyl wallet with the telephone number of their uncle's house in Iran written on a torn edge of newspaper, and the mobile phone number of the nephew of the tailor who was living in England.
* Two twenty-euro notes, which is all his Iranian money came to when Mohamed changed it for him in Istanbul.
* One photograph, folded once, of him and his brothers posing with their parents and their grandfather, taken by an aid worker his father once knew in Afghanistan, many years ago, before Kabir was born.
* One notebook with sketches from along the journey, and the bits of Afghan poems that come back to him, and, on a scrap of paper, an address in Rome that Ahmed in the sewing factory gave them before they left.
* One pen he found on the footpath in Istanbul beside a man selling lottery tickets.
* One last piece of chewing gum rolled up in silver paper.
* One red mobile phone without a SIM card – thrown away to remove any sign they have crossed through Turkey.

He feels for his belt. Inside it, stitched between the layers of leather, the last of their travel money.

The hours slip by. Aryan cannot tell if he has dozed or slept.

The road is growing rougher. The big tyres lurch into the potholes. The wind that accompanied them on the highway has dropped.

Finally they stop. Kabir sits up. Aryan's stomach tightens. He hears the sound of men's voices outside.

The doors swing open. For the first time he sees the driver, his dark bulk silhouetted against a pale rectangle of sky. He is a big man with short-cropped bottlebrush hair, small eyes in a ruddy face.

Aryan blinks in the pastel light, sees the smudge of blue hills beyond, wonders if it is dawn or dusk. The smell of cold and oxygen and the outside world invade the truck's fuggy cave.

Looming in the doorframe, the man searches, then points to Kabir.

'You, come,' he says.

The men in the truck stand up. Maybe this is the drop-off place for Patras. Kabir doesn't move.

'No, no,' the man says. 'Just the two brothers.'

He lunges at Kabir, and grabs him by the arm.

Kabir yowls as the man swings him over the edge of the truck and on to the ground. Aryan hurls himself behind him like a creature gone wild.

Hamid kicks over the boxes and throws himself after Aryan.

The driver catches Hamid hard with his fist and sends him sprawling backwards on to a tower of boxes that topple against the truck's inside wall. Then he slams the doors shut.

For a few moments all is silent; then Hamid is shouting and banging on the truck's metal sides. Somebody stifles his protests.

Outside, a thickset man is gripping Kabir by his arms. A white singlet stretches over his belly and a piece of rope holds up his trousers. He looks at the driver with nervous eyes, while the boy twists like a pinioned kitten in his grasp.

'Here's your merchandise,' the driver says to the Greek man. He nods.

The driver hoists himself into the cabin with a movement surprisingly lithe for a heavy man. He sends a rosary and a pair of dice swinging madly above the dashboard as he reverses back up the road.

Aryan runs after the truck, feet skidding in the mud as he loses his balance and recovers it beside the churning wheels. He thumps the vehicle's side.

'Hamid!' he shouts.

'Aryan!' comes the muffled reply.

The wheels spin and gain traction. The truck accelerates, and disappears over the rise.

Only when Aryan comes back does the man release the child.

Aryan pulls Kabir towards him and folds his arms across his brother's chest, holding him tight to stop his shaking. Kabir rubs his arms where the man's grip is already starting to flower into a purple tattoo of bruising.

The air is pungent with earth and manure. Ragged farm buildings sprawl around a rusting tractor abandoned in the yard. It has Greek lettering across the windscreen and its tyres have herringboned the soil like army tanks. Ploughed fields recede in the failing light, and, behind the rotting slats of an enclosure, pigs with mud-caked ankles root around an overturned pail.

Beyond them, the sky hangs low over a wide valley with bare, undulating hills. Aryan shivers as the breeze that has swept over Hamid's truck reaches him bereft of any message. It must be nightfall, he thinks, but he cannot remember which day.

'Where are we, Aryan?' Kabir says.

Aryan's tired mind is whirring. He is trying to recall whether Mohamed said anything about working in Greece when they set off from Istanbul. Surely he would have remembered. In the village near the Evros, the father of the boy with the withered arm said only that the truck would take them far across the border. He thought they were going to Patras, where all the Afghans were.

On bowlegs, the man in the singlet approaches.

'Come with me,' he says, his knobbled fist in the small of Aryan's back.

They are inside a small white building. Two pallets of straw fill the recess of a whitewashed concrete ledge. There is peeling green linoleum underfoot, and a dripping tap outside. A washed-out curtain hangs across the doorway, sagging in the places where it has torn through its hooks. Across the yard, smoke leaks upwards from the farmhouse chimney and smears the darkening sky. Their breath curls like writing in the air and disappears. In the outhouse there is no fireplace nor any source of heat.

'Wait.' The man crosses the yard and disappears inside the house.

Presently an old woman in black woollen stockings emerges. She wears a dark-blue apron whose pocket is torn and carries a tray with bread, two slabs of white cheese, and two bowls of broth. She has barnacles on her face like the nodes insects make under bark. Silently she sets the tray down on an upended log outside the building, scarcely looking at them. She shuffles back across the yard in shoes of cloth folded under at the heels like slippers.

The tap squeaks as Aryan washes Kabir's hands, then his own. The water comes out in a thin, twisted ribbon. There is almost no pressure. Aryan takes off his T-shirt and wets it and scrubs Kabir's face and ears and neck. The water splashes their feet and leaves spidery tributaries in the soil.

They have eaten nothing since Turkey. Aryan thinks of the pigs and does not touch the soup. But Kabir is too ravenous to hold back.

'It doesn't taste of anything, Aryan,' Kabir says. 'Just salt.'

Aryan sniffs the bowl. There is no sign of meat of any kind. 'Maybe it's just vegetables,' he says.

The rising steam and the sight of his brother eating are too much. Aryan lifts the bowl and sips gingerly, his hollow stomach contracting. There is none of the richness of lamb or goat or chicken, none of what he imagines would be pork. There is just hot water with coins of yellow oil on the surface, and grains of rice among the crescent moons of celery beneath.

They lick the grains from the bottom of their bowls, and demolish the bread and the last crumbs of the sour-tasting cheese. The liquid warms them, but when they have finished their hunger hasn't gone away.

Aryan leans back on the pallet. Lying down stretches his stomach flat, he tells himself; that way he won't feel so empty.

'I don't like it here,' Kabir says after a while.

'Well it's not my idea of paradise either,' Aryan says.

'Where do you think we are?'

'Somewhere in Greece, I suppose. We could be anywhere.'

'Why did they bring us here?'

'I don't know, Kabir. I guess it's to work.'

'Doing what?'

'Probably farm work.'

'Why didn't Hamid come too?'

'Maybe they only need two people.'

'How long do we have to stay?'

'Kabir, I have no idea. Probably till we've earned our passage and they are ready to move us on.'

Aryan is suddenly tired of his little brother. He is tired of having to think for the two of them. Tired of being held back by his brother's short legs. Tired of having to be reassuring when he is riddled with foreboding. Tired of having to provide answers to things he doesn't understand.

Then immediately he feels guilty. On the long walk over the mountains between Iran and Turkey Kabir had hardly complained, though his jeans were chafing and their feet were on fire in the rocky terrain and their mouths were sandpaper dry. Aryan was amazed that he didn't protest and just kept walking as fast as he could so the smugglers wouldn't hit him with their guns. It was only later that Aryan saw how thin his sneakers had become after all that shredding on the rocks. Kabir can't help asking questions – he's always been like that – and with Hamid gone, he will have no one but Aryan to ask.

'What about Hamid?' Kabir says as if on cue. 'Do you think he's got any injuries?'

Aryan sighs. 'He might be a bit sore,' he says. 'You heard him hollering in the back of the truck.'

'He might have a good black bruise,' Kabir says.

'Or a big black eye.'

'Or two black eyes and a bruise.'

'Well maybe not all of them,' Aryan says.

Hamid is tough, Aryan knows. Tougher than he is. He is impetuous and his temper gets him into trouble but he is also fearless, and quick to seize an opportunity. A Tajik, he made it all the way to Istanbul on his own after fleeing the Taliban; Aryan has always been a little in awe. He also felt they made a team, he and Hamid and Kabir. It was Hamid who led them through the steep streets of Istanbul to watch the tankers gliding past the minarets along the Bosporus, and used them as decoys while he filched pastries from café tables so they could devour them, out of sight, in the twisting alleys. With a rush Aryan misses him, and feels unsteady without him, aware that all the decisions he will have to make for him and Kabir he will now have to take on his own.

'Why didn't they let Hamid stay with us?' Kabir says.

'Why do you keep asking questions I cannot answer?' says Aryan.

There are times when Aryan wonders if he shouldn't have left Kabir behind. He could have stayed with their cousins in Iran and Aryan would have sent for him once he made it to Europe. But after everything that had happened Kabir was distraught at the idea of separation. And Aryan hadn't known how long it would be before Kabir could join him, and in the end he had put together the money from all the things he had sold, and relented.

But now he wishes he could be alone to think. He doesn't understand why they were thrown off the truck, or why they were separated from the others. He is starting to wonder whether some arrangement hasn't been made concerning them – in Istanbul, maybe, or by the people who took them across the river to Greece.

Kabir turns his back. His frustration ripples through the silence in invisible waves. Aryan knows he has hurt his feelings, but for the moment he doesn't care.

Since they arrived, something unexplained has been flickering at the back of Aryan's mind. Now it rises towards the surface like a diving bird swimming upwards through the waters of a lake, and formulates itself into a question.

How did the driver know they were brothers?

A thumbnail moon hangs in the darkening sky and a pale light emanates from one of the windows in the house. It is too cold to undress. Aryan doubles one of the blankets over the straw pallet and makes Kabir crawl inside. Aryan folds the other blankets over the top of him, and spreads their anoraks over his shoulders. Then he huddles under the covers beside him and hugs his brother to keep them both warm.

With a start he realizes Kabir is crying.

'Hey, what's wrong, Soldierboy?' Aryan says.

Kabir is silent.

'Tell me,' Aryan says.

He doesn't respond.

'Is this the brother who was strong enough to cross the desert and the mountains, like Rostam in the stories Baba used to read to us back home?' Aryan says.

The boy sniffs wetly.

'You can't be sad for no reason. Tell me what's wrong.'

'I want to go back,' Kabir says after a while.

'Back where?'

'Back to Iran. Back to our cousins' place. Back to Zohra and Masood.'

Aryan sighs. 'Me too,' he says. 'But we can't go back now, Kabir.'

'Why not?'

'Not after what we've spent to get this far. They'd laugh at us, and then they'd be ashamed. Everyone would say we were cowards.'

'I don't care,' Kabir says. 'I hate it here.'

'I don't like it either, but you were the one who insisted on coming. You knew it was going to be tough. Anyway, I thought you wanted to go to school.'

'I do. But we're in Europe now and I can't see any schools.'

'That's why we're going to England.'

'Why don't we go there then? Why do we have to stay here?'

'It'll be like Istanbul. First we have to work and then they will put us on a truck,' Aryan says.

'How long will we have to stay?'

'I didn't even know we were coming here, Kabir. But if it's like in Turkey, maybe we will have to stay a few months.'

Exhaustion bears down on Aryan like an edifice. He desperately wants to succumb, and let oblivion sweep his worries back across all the plains, back across all the mountains and plateaux and villages and cities and roads and checkpoints and borders and rivers and deserts that they have crossed. The frisson of elation he felt when they got to Europe has retreated under a new layer of anxiety. He supposes that it will be months before he can really relax, sleep deeply, and not awaken with worry about money or time or how far they are from their goal, or how they will manage the next step. He wishes their father were still alive, or that he could speak to Omar back there in Iran, or to some adult who would know what to do.

He hears Kabir's breathing steady, and soon slips over the soft cliff of unconsciousness too.

Sometime in the middle of the night, Kabir whips the blankets off.

'Something bit me,' he says.

'Where?' Aryan peers at his brother's shape in the dimness. 'I can't see anything.'

Then he feels it himself. The sudden sting. The burn. The itch.

He leaps to his feet, and tosses the blankets to the floor. Aryan pushes Kabir towards the window. He inspects his torso, sees nothing. Then he discovers an angry weal flowering on his rib.

Then he sees two more. And then two on his own leg.

He gives Kabir one corner of the blanket to hold.

'Higher!' he says. Kabir is too short and half of it crumples on the floor. There is an old rake leaning against the wall. Aryan grabs it and, holding the other end of the blanket, uses it to beat the cloth. They do it for all four blankets, and sweep the mattress clear with their hands.

'Try not to scratch,' Aryan says. 'Put saliva on it where it is itchy. We will ask for different bedding in the morning.'

They try again to sleep, jumpy with real and imagined insects every time the blanket moves. It prickles with their body heat.

After a while Kabir's breathing deepens. Aryan listens to it for a long time.

Hours later Aryan loses the debate with himself and gets up to go outside. Kabir doesn't stir as he pushes the curtain aside.

He pees against the side of the outhouse, folds his arms around himself, and lingers in the cold night air. Stillness enfolds the land and the sky is alive with stars. One hanging low on the horizon is so bright it hurts his eyes. Somewhere a farm dog barks, and another answers. A shooting star streaks swift as rocket fire across the heavens.

He gazes up the road where their truck disappeared. Even if they could run away, there are no trees in this bald land, no forest, no place to hide. He doesn't know from what direction they have come, let alone which direction to take.

He thinks about Hamid and wonders where he is now. He misses his daring and his jokes, tries to imagine what he would do if he were here.

In the morning when the old woman comes they show her the bites and ask for new blankets. She looks fiercely at them and barks something in Greek they don't understand.

She sets down a tray with cheese and some pieces of cucumber and sweetened black tea in mugs. She returns to the house and flicks the curtain shut behind her.

Aryan follows her to the door and waits. He blows on his hands to warm his fingers, then hugs them under his armpits. She doesn't come out again.

In their outhouse, Kabir has left him half the food. Aryan notices his face still shows the creases where he has slept on the edge of the blanket. He cradles the mug of tea in his hands, trying to coax its warmth into his fingers.

Suddenly they hear the sound of an engine. The farmer's old pick-up truck is idling in the yard.

'Get in,' the farmer says. He is leaning out the half-opened door. 'Today we go to another place.'

Aryan hesitates. 'What other place?' he says.

'For working,' the farmer says. 'Many trees.'

30

The dashboard is cracked from the sun and covered in dust but the clock still works, even if the time shown by its glow-in-the-dark hands can't be right. There is no heating in the truck; Kabir leans into Aryan for warmth.

They drive for over an hour, watching the landscape change. The earth becomes stonier and redder. They pass groves of stunted olive trees, the trunks spaced evenly as chessmen. Aryan half-closes his eyes; the winter trees flicker light-dark, light-dark through his eyelids as they pass. Bamboo thickets shiver along the roadsides. Plastic-sheeted hothouses dot the desolate landscape; idle watering systems poise angular as stick insects in the fields. In the distance, the mountains are hard and white, not like the ochre ridges that dissolved in the rains where he was born. The road signs are all in two languages, English characters beneath strange Greek symbols, but Aryan doesn't recognize any words.

They turn into a bumpy dirt road that leads to an orchard. The trees are dark and laden with golden orbs.

The farmer tears at the handbrake.

Outside the truck, the air is cold and still. Though the sun has finally risen, a lacework of frost still decorates the dead leaves on the ground. Aryan jogs on the spot to warm his feet, like they did before Omar's games. Kabir is blowing on his hands.

A couple of ladders lean on their sides against a low stone wall. There is a shed with wooden crates; more tumble in a pile outside it. A blue tarpaulin flattens the grass where it lies, rolled up under the trees.

The farmer pulls one of the ladders upright; it squeals as he kicks its feet apart and plants them in the soft soil. He pulls the tarpaulin round its base, then climbs up to show them how.

He twists the oranges off the branches and drops them into a bag slung across his chest. Loosened fruit fall like outsized hailstones on to the sheet below.

He passes the bag to Aryan; Kabir's job is to collect the falling oranges, fill the crates and stack them along the wall, and to pull the fruit from the branches he can reach from the ground.

At the top of the ladder, Aryan leans into the foliage. Before him the luminous spheres are white with frost; they hang from the branches like planets under their polar caps. Waxy leaves slap him in the face as the too-heavy fruits resist, then suddenly give.

The watery sunshine releases a faint tanginess from the leaves that immediately wafts out of reach. Quickly Aryan's fingers grow red and numb and wet from handling the frozen globes. He drops his arms to his sides to let the blood flow back, then squeezes his hands under his armpits. He hangs his head to ease the muscle-ache in his neck.

Later, when the farmer has retreated to the end of the property, Aryan half-slides down the ladder to rest. With blunt fingers he tears open an orange from a lower branch. The skin is thick and easy to peel; inside, capsules of sweetness rear up like feathers. Their teeth jar with the citric cold as they melt the icy segments in their mouths. There is nothing of the sourness of the oranges they had back home.

Aryan tries to concentrate on the flavour, probing with his tongue the bits of fibre caught between his teeth as he tries to remember what the taste reminds him of. He blows the pips at Kabir, and they skiffle pieces of skin into the grass as if they were pebbles on the surface of a lake.

Kabir tries to peel a whole orange into a word in Afghan writing but the loops break apart in his hands. He wears stickiness from his eyebrows to his chin.

'The ants will be after you,' Aryan says.

Kabir wipes his shiny face on his sleeve. 'No they won't,' he says with a grin. 'They're hibernating.'

The farmer shouts and Aryan scurries back up the ladder. The man yells insults and scowls at him from the foot of the tree.

As he works Aryan tries to identify a memory that hovers like a dragonfly just out of reach. He explores the recesses of his mind, then lets it go blank, pretending he is not searching for anything at all, just pulling and reaching and pulling the fruit from the recalcitrant trees. And then it comes to him.

The house when he was small. A celebration. Sitting altogether under the tree-trunk beams of the ceiling. His father coming in from the bazaar, emptying his pockets of the cigarette lighters and batteries and the mobile phones he hawked in the street after he lost his post at the school. Aunts and uncles and cousins crowding into the small room. His grandfather making his way through them, favouring his aching joints, washing his hands in an enamel bowl and drying them on a white cloth. The blind television under its rug in the corner, its jump leads disconnected from the battery. His cousin Zohra and their mother were passing around a deep ceramic bowl filled with pomegranate seeds. There were mandarins, too, and grapes that exploded with sugar, the sweetest fruits he had ever tasted. A long time ago, before they left Afghanistan.

At nightfall they stuff oranges into their anoraks in case they get hungry later on.

It is still dark when the long blast of a horn awakens them the next morning. The icy air is filled with petrol fumes as the farmer waits behind the wheel. The hogs in their enclosure grunt their disapproval at his headlights.

Aryan catches a glimpse of the farmer's watch as he works the gear-stick. It says four thirty a.m.

In the pre-dawn darkness the oranges gleam like silver cricket balls.

Rows of trees stretch out before them. Up in the leaf canopy Aryan fills the bag and lowers it to Kabir. It is so heavy he has to watch it doesn't tip him off balance as he

34

descends. He feels the legs of the ladder sinking into the soil as he shifts his weight.

Kabir scurries to gather the fruit that escape on to the tarpaulin. He rolls them like giant marbles when the farmer is out of sight, before packing them into the crates. Aryan leans into the top rung of the ladder as he works, periodically stopping to rub the metal dents out of his knees.

Though it's cold in the orchard, the work gives them a raging thirst. They have no water so they suck the juice from the oranges, but the sweetness just makes it worse.

Sometimes, at the far end of the orchard, other men show up to strip the trees. Taciturn, they come by the shed from time to time to pick up more crates before hurrying back to work. Their clothes are grubby and their faces are dark like they haven't had time to sleep; and they move fast to fill the containers. Once Aryan called out to one of them, but he couldn't understand the language of the reply.

The men light a fire among the orange trees and thaw their hands over the warmth. Aryan and Kabir can smell the smoke weaving between the branches but the flames are too distant for them to share.

Every night in the truck on the way back to the farm, Kabir collapses into Aryan's shoulder, falling into a sleep from which not even the potholes can rouse him.

They harvest oranges even in the rain.

Hands mottled with cold, Aryan zips Kabir into his anorak. Their clothes are too thin, and the leaves slap water into their faces and down their necks. The rungs of the ladder turn slippery in the wet.

Kabir complains. The hard fabric of his anorak chafes his chin and rubs it raw.

In the mid-afternoon drizzle, Aryan stretches for a branch just out of reach. His weight shifts on the ladder, and its front foot digs deep into the earth, leaning it sideways. As his shoe searches its way along the metal rung, the orange comes away suddenly in his hand and the branch slaps back into his face. Blinded, he loses his grip, and falls.

He lands heavily on his ankle, yelping with pain. Kabir drops his crate, oranges bouncing like lottery balls, and comes running.

Nostrils flared, Aryan is breathing hard. He rolls from side to side on the blue tarpaulin, one knee hard up against his chest. Electric currents of pain shoot through his leg.

'Tell the farmer,' he says through clenched teeth.

They drive home in silence. Aryan's ankle has swollen like a marrow. He can hardly keep on his shoe.

When he is lying on his freezing pallet, the old woman brings him aspirin so old that the blue writing on the tinfoil wrapping has almost worn away. It fizzes and dies in the water at the bottom of a chipped china cup.

She also brings him ice in a kitchen cloth. Aryan winces as she lays it on the swelling.

'I can't work tomorrow,' Aryan tells the farmer.

The man frowns. 'We'll dock it from your pay.'

In a week they go back to the orchard. Aryan walks gingerly, testing the ligaments. The swelling has gone down, but he is afraid to trust his ankle with his full weight. The oranges glow like suns against the blue winter sky.

Up the ladder again he leans into the branches, trying to concentrate, despite the cold that deadens his hands, on not falling.

In the middle of the afternoon there is a plop-plopping on the leaves. It starts to rain.

One evening, the farmer comes to see them after he has driven them back to the house and they are washing their hands under the protesting tap. He is wearing a sweater that zips up at the neck.

'One week's work,' he says, putting a scroll of cash into Aryan's dripping hand. Then he goes back indoors.

Aryan unrolls the bills and counts them. Two gold fifty-euro notes, one blue twenty-euro note, a tattered five-euro note, plus one euro coin.

He counts them again, the notes making a nest as Aryan lays them on the bed, placing the silver coin in the middle like an egg.

'We're rich,' Kabir says with a grin.

Aryan ignores him. 'I think he's made a mistake,' he says. 'A hundred and twenty-six euros isn't right. Ahmed said you could make fifteen euros a day on the farms in Greece.'

He pauses to calculate, and writes the numbers in his notebook to make sure.

'It should be two hundred and ten euros for the two of us,' he says.

Outside the house Aryan stops a moment, and swallows. He is not used to having to stand up to people. Hamid, he knows, wouldn't hesitate. His ankle is starting to throb, but thinking about Hamid helps to steel him, and anger about being cheated propels him.

He knocks on the wooden doorframe. The door is shut but a corner of the curtain is caught in the jamb like the petticoat of someone in a rush. The farmer opens up immediately – he must have been leaning against the inside of it to take off his boots. He squints at Aryan with squirrel eyes.

Aryan can smell woodsmoke and charcoal and onions and his stomach concertinas with hunger.

'This isn't the right amount,' he says, holding out the notes. His hand is shaking. 'It should be fifteen euros a day.'

'No,' the farmer says. 'Not fifteen. Fifteen is the price for a man. You are only a boy and boys don't do the work of a man.'

Aryan flushes. 'I know the price is fifteen,' he says.

'I give you ten euros,' the farmer says. 'Ten is a very good price – and on top of that I give you bed and food. That costs me money that I am paying for you!'

Aryan's throat tightens. 'I work hard for you, as hard as a man, and you should pay me the same price,' he says.

'And where are you going to sleep? Where will you have a bed, food, shelter? Where are you going to find these conditions? You think these things are free? In Greece life is very expensive; no one will let you stay as cheaply as me. You don't have any idea how much a hotel costs. Then you need transport. You will have to pay for a bus, then walk, and now your ankle is weak. Ten euros is a good price, you don't know how good it is.'

Aryan reflects for a moment. What the man says is true – they don't know where they are or where else they can go, or what they would have to pay to sleep elsewhere. At least he is giving them some money, even if it's less than he should. He does some fast calculations. Ten euros a day for seven days is a hundred and forty euros for the two of them, yet still the man has only paid a hundred and twenty-six.

'What about my brother? He works hard too. You say ten euros a day but this money is not ten euros a day,' Aryan says. 'We are two.' Aryan clenches his hand in his pocket, as if extra courage were to be found in the threadbare cloth.

'Your brother, he is too small,' the farmer says, eyes glowering under heavy brows. 'He can't do the work of a man either. He only plays all the time. For him I pay eight euros a day. And that's a good price.'

'My brother works hard. He is all day with me, collecting oranges, putting them in crates, dragging them to the wall. You pay him the same as me, ten euros a day exactly,' Aryan says.

The man laughs. 'This boy your brother, he is no use to me. I could take one man and get the work done three times as fast as I do with you two boys. I'm doing you a favour by letting you work here. But maybe you don't want to work at all. Maybe you don't want to wait for the truck to Italy,' he says.

'When is the truck coming?' Aryan says.

'Only when the work is done,' the farmer says.

Kabir is lying on the pallet with his shoes on when Aryan returns. The floor is covered in footprints like the dance-steps of ghosts.

'What happened?' Kabir says.

Aryan shoves his brother's feet off the bed. 'Take your shoes off first,' he says.

Kabir puts his feet back.

'Have it your way,' Aryan says. 'Sleep like those pigs do in the dirt.'

Aryan flops down on the other pallet. His arms and legs feel heavy. His head is tired and his ankle hurts.

'So what did he say?' Kabir asks.

'Nothing,' Aryan says.

'He must have said something.'

'There's no more money. He is paying less because we

are not men, and less for you because you are only a kid and spend all day mucking around.'

'That's not true,' Kabir says. 'I work hard too.'

'He says because we get this place to sleep and food at night then I only get ten and you only get eight because you are too slow.'

'But you said we could get fifteen!' Kabir says. 'Let's go somewhere else.'

'And where would you like to go? We don't even know where we are right now. At least here there is a truck to Italy.'

'When?'

'When the work is finished, the farmer said.'

'And when's that?'

Aryan shrugs. 'When there are no more oranges, I suppose.'

Every day they leave the farm hours before sunrise and drive in the battered pick-up truck to the orchard in order to start work before dawn. Sometimes they are so tired they don't even hear the engine running. The farmer leans his impatience into the horn.

Aryan reckons it's been six weeks since they arrived. He marks down the days in his notebook with four lines and a stroke, the way his father showed him, to make them easier to count.

The oranges have been harvested, but there is still more

work on the farm. The grass is no longer furry with ice crystals in the mornings; there is a shy warmth in the sun in the middle of the day.

There are rows and rows of potatoes to dig up. Then there will be turnips. And then onions that need to be pulled by nimble hands.

They are given digging forks, and green plastic crates to fill.

Other men come to work on the farm but Aryan only sees them in the distance. They stoop over the furrows, unkempt hair in their eyes. A tractor crawls across the land like a rusted scorpion; trucks back up to the gate for loading.

By the end of the day the pads of Aryan's hands are tender with blisters. Kabir's nails are black from grubbing out the roots in the soil Aryan has overturned; smears of dirt mark his face with warpaint.

In the mornings, the wind bores straight at them over the hill; they have to keep working to keep warm.

The farmer comes to see them during the afternoon. He wades into the furrows like a bulldog, the same rope holding up his trousers.

Aryan decides to ask him why, except that once, they haven't been paid.

'I changed my mind,' the farmer says. 'If I give you cash you have to keep it somewhere. You will lose it in the fields or it will get stolen. It's better if you work to pay the next part of your journey.'

Aryan swallows. 'How long will that take?'

'You work hard here, and soon you will be on your way.'

'But when?' Aryan insists. 'How many more weeks?'

'Just a few,' the man says. 'Less if you work hard. Then you will get on your truck.'

The fields stretch away down the valley. Aryan thinks it will be more than just a few weeks.

Aryan's blisters harden to calluses. His shoulders burn from the digging. Kabir grows silent, the mischief absent from his eyes.

'It was better in the sewing factory, wasn't it,' Aryan says.

He can still feel the air vibrate with the incessant hum of the needles, the stifling heat as they bent over the noisy machines. The rucking of fabric he had to take care not to stain with his sweating hands. They blinked and squinted at the material under light bulbs roped to the ceiling with cobwebs. There were five rows of men from different places, from Afghanistan, Iraq, and distant parts of Turkey, who couldn't all communicate with each other.

Mohamed liked Afghans. 'Afghans are very good workers,' he used to say, surveying his factory floor.

Ahmed was one of them. He kept an eye out for Aryan and Kabir, and explained how things worked in Greece, and gave them an address in Rome of an Afghan man if ever they needed help. Aryan kept the paper safe in his wallet, then copied it into the pages of his notebook, between the sketches he sometimes did of people or the places they'd seen, where he kept important things.

It was Ahmed who introduced them to Hamid. Hamid worked next door, in another of Mohamed's factories, cutting pieces of leather for shoes. His workshop reeked of animal skins and the choking stench of dyes.

There were mornings when some of the men had left without warning and a new team would already have arrived to replace them. One day, Aryan supposed, Ahmed too would be gone.

Kabir was the youngest in the workroom. While Aryan sewed he collected the offcuts of cloth, refilled the holders when the spools ran out, and chased the threads and scraps and tumbleweeds of dust into sacks with a long-handled broom. The men ruffled his hair and joked with him, hiding the empty bobbins and then producing them like magic from behind his ears.

Sometimes Aryan felt a stab of jealousy. Sometimes he would have liked to have been the centre of attention, everyone's favourite boy.

But here Aryan was treated like an adult. Every day he had hundreds of buttonholes to sew, stop-start, stop-start, his foot controlling the speed with a switch so sensitive that the merest touch would fling it on a hungry riff of its own. Once, at the beginning, he sewed up his fingers. With a lurch he remembers the needle's silver lick that had done its deed before he could even register the danger. He'd watched the white calligraphy slowly turn pink as if it were someone else's hand, the maroon dewdrops blooming like living things. Then, in the airless room, he'd nearly fainted. He was kept alert by a smack over the ear from the supervisor, who yanked out the threads with scissors.

He could still read the scribble of the needle's faint staccato on his skin.

They started at eight a.m. and didn't finish until nine at night. By the end of the day they did not even have the energy to watch the football games with the Turks on the television that they thwacked with a slipper whenever the picture fragmented. They never had enough to eat. But after thirteen weeks, Mohamed had kept his word.

'Tomorrow, at dawn, you go,' he had told them one night.

They had risen in the dark with the first call of the muezzin, and stood in the doorway waiting for his cousin to complete his prayers and roll up his mat, watching with identical sets of black eyes.

Then the cousin drove them from Istanbul to the mechanics' yard near the border in an old truck laden with spare tyres. Hamid was already in the back when they clambered on board.

Everything in the Internet café is black: the windows, the walls, the chairs, even the cubicles where rows of men sit, joystick in hand, heads bulbous as insects under shiny headphones, faces illuminated blue in the glow of the screen.

Every now and then there is a whoosh and a zing as someone's game comes screeching to an end. It is Hamid who has taken him there, who is standing on one side of him, while Kabir stands on the other, in the dark.

Aryan is sitting at station 21. He touches the keyboard and a box flips up asking for a password. Carefully, he copies in the word that the Turkish woman at the counter gave him on a piece of card. The keys stick to his fingertips, the plastic discoloured with dirt.

The word 'WELCOME' flips up in a box beside the face of a ticking clock. He has only paid for fifteen minutes and he knows from school in Iran how fast time disappears on the Web.

It takes several tries to drag the clock to the corner of the screen. The mouse has no traction on the laminated tabletop.

Thirteen minutes left.

Aryan bites his bottom lip in concentration.

He recognizes some of the symbols from the computer they used at school, and he clicks on to the familiar blue 'e'. In the blank space he types the word 'Evros', insisting on the letter 's' that is jammed with grime. Then he selects 'map' from the top of the screen.

A list comes up in Turkish; he trawls down till he can find some English lettering, and clicks.

There it is. The border.

Eleven minutes left.

The clock must be rigged.

He peers under the line of red markings at the river. It squeezes its way like a blue question mark between Turkey and Greece before fraying into a light-brown delta on the edge of the sea. 'Sanctuary,' he reads. There is a symbol for migratory birds.

He examines the green shading on either side of the question mark: the river's wide floodplain. One small bridge spans the watery expanse. Higher up, where the contours narrow along the question mark's curved back, he sees a line of yellow and black triangles. He down-arrows till he finds the legend.

Nine minutes to go.

The seconds are vanishing faster than water down a drain.

'Landmines.'

His breath catches. No one has said anything about landmines. He has seen what they could do to villagers back home, to kids who thought they were toys; it never occurred to him they might also have them in Europe.

He scrolls back up. The border zone looks very wide. He tries to measure it with his thumb against the scale at the bottom of the screen. Seven kilometres, maybe. On foot, and with variations in the terrain, it must be more.

Six minutes left.

He zooms in to enlarge the border crossing at Kipi. He guesses that the river is narrowest there if that's where

they decided to build a bridge. But it would be too dangerous for a pick-up on the road that fed the crossing and too
far to get to the highway beyond. His eye runs upstream;
further north, there are places where the highway in
Greece runs so close to the river that it looks like the two
of them touch. The bank there must be very steep, he
thinks, or the highway raised, otherwise the road would
flood. He wonders if there are trees or if it's open ground;
he can't tell from the map whether the land is rocky or
muddy or of clay.

Four minutes.

He looks for lettering. The last villages on the Turkish
side; the towns that control the borderlands in Greece:
Orestiada halfway up, Alexandroupoli right on the sea, the
small places in between: Feres, Tychero, Soufli, Didymoticho.
A river with two names: Evros, and Meric Nehri. He
wonders if they mean the same thing. And far beyond all of
them, green fading to brown, more mountains, tighter
contours, another country: Bulgaria.

WARNING: save data now! Your session will expire in two
minutes!

Print, he should try to print. There is no printer symbol
on the map page. Try the menu. Liberated from the cursor,
the tractionless mouse slides gaily over the desktop. He
shoves an Internet flyer beneath it till finally it engages,
then shoots the cursor to the top of the screen. A drop-
down menu appears, and then another. The words are all
in Turkish. He can't find the printer command.

THANK YOU: your session is now over!

Aryan drops his hands in defeat.

Whoosh. Zing. The boy in the next-door cubicle punches the air as he scores against the machine.

There is an old dog on the farm who follows them out to the fields.

Every day they go, even when it rains, and the old dog always goes with them. She is a mongrel, black and white, hopeful eyebrows raised above despondent eyes. She runs sideways like a crab from adult men, neck extended, shying away like a creature too often kicked. Kabir plays with her whenever he gets the chance, and she follows him around like a disciple.

Their clothes grow stiff with soil. They wear their anoraks when it rains but that doesn't stop the mud from caking their trousers.

Aryan goes to the house and mimes a request for a bucket. The old woman flicks the curtain behind her and disappears.

Kabir catches him up. He peers through the crack in the curtain and enumerates what he sees: potatoes covering the table, metal pans on hooks, tall saucepans steaming on a wood stove. There is a television screen covered with an old lace cloth.

He steps backwards.

The old lady is holding out a metal tub with handles at each end. Inside she has put a cake of cracked yellow soap.

Aryan fills the tub from the tap, scrubs Kabir's T-shirt and spreads it over the stone wall in the morning, waiting for the anaemic sun. In the meantime he lends Kabir his own, and laughs at the way it hangs off his shoulders like a dress.

Kabir's T-shirt lies out there for a whole day without drying.

Finally Aryan sets some old crates and a couple of fence palings alight. The T-shirt balloons over the fire like a sail. Kabir's body heat finishes off the drying process; for the next two days he trails the scent of smoke.

They can never get their hands completely clean. Their calluses have grown yellow and thick. Their fingernails are circles etched in dark, indelible dye.

For lunch the old woman gives them black tea and bread. At night they get transparent soup with strips of cabbage in it. They always feel hungry at the end.

Aryan has a sudden longing for the pomegranate juice they used to get in season back home. He tries to remember the taste, the dark-pink sweetness. The last time he drank it was in Istanbul, when Ahmed in the factory brought them a glass, walking slowly, his workman's paw cupping the rim like a chalice of rubies.

At first Aryan hid a few of the smaller potatoes in his pocket. When they were hungry at night they ate them raw, but they made their stomachs cramp.

Now, when they rise before dawn, the air smells different. It is something Aryan recognizes from home: the tingle of life stirring under the soil as winter gives way to spring.

One day the dog doesn't follow them into the fields. Kabir is distraught.

'Old Dog! Old Dog!' he calls, but the familiar haunches do not appear.

Two days later he finds her in a rusting barrel at the back of the machine shed. At her side, two pups are nuzzling her teats.

'Maybe she wasn't so old after all,' Aryan says.

Kabir can't stop smiling. When the pups are strong enough to walk, their mother brings them with her to the field to watch the boys uproot the potato plants. He rolls a potato towards them and watches them bat it around like kittens with a freshly killed mouse.

Kabir's laughter fills the entire field as the old dog teaches the puppies to dig. They send the earth flying and fall over, legs pedalling each other like cyclists. He can't understand why the dirt doesn't stick to the pink-and-brown pads under their feet. They follow their noses in loops along invisible maps and pat at worms and roll around in the soil the boys overturn.

Kabir calls them Tom and Jerry after the cartoon characters they saw in a book in Iran. He saves his bread and feeds them pieces that they nudge from his hand with their noses and the flick of soft tongues. They lie on their backs with their paws in the air, offering their velvet underbellies. He carries them around on his shoulders and giggles when they lick his ears.

He drops them from a height to see if they will land on their feet and laughs when they yelp in shock.

Aryan clips him on the ear for his cruelty.

It is roughly then that the bad dreams start to come back.

There has been a rocket attack on the market. The world is dim and Aryan is wading through a haze of dust. His hair is wet and he is staggering across the dry riverbed, to the place where the market used to be. A girl is dragging herself on her hands through the debris, a white bone poking out of her leg. There is blood all over the apples.

Aryan is searching, searching, but there are no bodies left, just pieces of bodies, and apples everywhere, and blood seeping into the sand.

He knows he is there, but he can't find his father anywhere. His uncle orders him to keep looking.

He wakes up, heaving.

One morning Kabir gets out of bed, black eyes shiny as oil, and throws up. Afterwards, he is too weak to stand.

Aryan knows without the farmer's telling them that this is one day more they will have to stay.

Aryan sits by Kabir all day. When he shivers, Aryan wraps him in their blankets. When he sweats, he pushes water to his lips in an enamel cup.

Kabir can't even hold the water down.

His face is hot and his hair sticks to his forehead. Aryan wets his T-shirt and washes his brother's face. He observes the soft profile a long time, the round cheeks flushed with fever, the eyebrows black against pallid skin, and his heart constricts.

The old woman brings a jug of water with salt and sugar in it from the house. The grains lie insoluble as sand on the bottom.

'I'm so thirsty,' Kabir mutters. But the water just reactivates the retching. It is not until the afternoon that Aryan can get him to take a few sips. His fingerprints evaporate in slow-shrinking clouds on the glass.

He sleeps. Aryan leans against the wall beside him, listening to the shallow breathing. Outside, the hills turn blue and soften in the twilight. Far away, across the valley, the smudge of another village; at night, faint pinpricks of light wink across the darkness.

Sometimes Kabir talks in his sleep. Long incoherent ramblings. Sometimes he asks about Ali, about what happened to Bashir. Sometimes their mother. Sometimes it's the Kurdish horsemen who frightened him so much. Sometimes he asks for Hamid, and mumbles about the day they set out to explore Istanbul.

'You can't leave Istanbul without having seen the

Golden Horn,' Hamid had said, and he had led them on a merry dance, propelling them down the vertiginous streets to the filthy Bosporus, leaping on and off the crowded ferries, cruising past the palaces and towers and mosques, pinching candied fruit from the bazaars and rings of sesame bread from the market stalls under the bridges. He took them to the Blue Mosque where they peeled off their shoes and lay on a sea of carpets and gazed up at the stained glass windows. They slipped into a palace where sultans once lived to admire daggers encrusted with emeralds.

Aryan never learned how Hamid first found his way down to the water, and back through the maze of streets to the hole in the wall where he worked – nor how he did it without Mohamed finding out. He just seemed to have a flair for risk. Or maybe Mohamed had grown fond of Hamid and simply turned a blind eye.

On the second day Kabir looks a little better, and the retching stops. He sleeps nearly all day long. To pass the time Aryan takes his notebook and sketches his brother's face, then sketches him from memory playing with the puppies in the field.

Then it is Aryan's turn.

Fever, sweating. His skin itches under the blankets. He can't sleep. He is cold then hot. He shivers and sweats. He can't hold anything down.

Sometimes Kabir is beside him. He remembers the

puppies playing at his feet, the sound of lapping as they drank water from the old pan Kabir found lying in the yard.

He dreams. There is strangeness and violence but no conclusions.

They are back on the Turkish border, crossing the river. They are in a boat that is leaking, but they have nearly reached the shore. There are soldiers among the trees ahead of them. More come out up and down the banks. He can see the silhouettes of their guns, and there is nowhere to land. Water fills the front of the dinghy which is heavy with the weight of men. Aryan is scared that the soldiers will shoot them, or shoot holes in the boat and they will drown. The boatman flails with the pole, trying to turn back. But the dancing lights on the bridge are spreading out, bobbing through the trees, getting closer on the shore they have just left. Hamid is with them in the boat. 'We've got to swim,' he says, and leans over the writhing current. 'Come on!' But Kabir won't jump and Aryan will not leave him. Suddenly the boatman strikes the bottom, the dinghy skids sideways, and there's a splash. Hamid's head is bobbing in the water as the current ferries him downstream. There is a shot, and a burning sensation, and Aryan is bleeding from his side.

Other dreams take its place. He is in Afghanistan again, and somehow he already knows what is coming because he has dreamt it before. There is dust everywhere and the mangled half-body of a car. Half of the street has disappeared; it looks like the mouth of a friend with the teeth knocked out. The police station wall has collapsed on to a watermelon stall and the fruit have split like skulls, spilling their red pulp over the road. There are slicks of blood as black as engine grease, and people dragging the injured into doorways. Rescuers are trying to lever up the fallen masonry; he can hear the sound of moaning like an animal caught in a trap. And then even the moaning stops. When he gets close he recognizes the sensible shoes, and the clothes under the blood-soaked burka.

What he can't understand is why the foot in the shoe is not attached to his mother's body any more.

Suddenly he is in the street outside the house in Tehran. His mother is in the doorway holding Kabir. Aryan is going to school and the bigger boys are waiting for him. They don't like Afghans in their neighbourhood. There is a maths test and he has stayed up half the night to prepare for it. They are lurking with slingshots in the alleyway. A stone the size of a walnut hits him in the heart.

The layers of danger mingle with pictures so fantastical that later he can't distinguish which ones were real.

They are back in Istanbul and have stolen away once more with Hamid. They are inside a giant mosque with a dome made of a million gold mosaics. Viking warriors are leaning out over the balcony, looking down into the biggest building they have ever seen. Their knife-blades flash as they carve Nordic graffiti into the stone. On the walls, high above the gaping Norsemen, are pictures of people with peaceful faces making strange Christian signs with their hands. Only the hardest-to-reach faces are left; the others have been chiselled away. The three of them, he, Hamid and Kabir, are looking up at them from beneath the highest dome. There is a flapping in the rafters, and a pigeon splices the shafts of sunlight, pale feathers golden in the slanting sun. Then, with no announcement, a single mosaic falls, and then another, and another, and the bird claps an incantation of dust and then hundreds of golden squares are tumbling down beside them and all around them – a waterfall of ancient tiles of glass shimmering and flashing as they fall in slow revolutions, splintering on the flagstones in a tinkling kaleidoscope of light.

Aryan doesn't know how long he is like this, drifting between fever and nightmare and fantasy and memory and sleep.

When he starts to come out of it, Kabir and the puppies bring him a hard-boiled egg.

Afterwards, they go back to the fields, Aryan, Kabir, and the three dogs. Kabir's puffy cheeks are white and Aryan's limbs feel leaden in the sunlight.

Aryan scores the passing days in the notebook that he rarely has time to sketch in now. The big potato fields are nearly finished, the scraggly stalks ripped from the soil and stuffed into rubbish sacks, the speckled nuggets salvaged from the sheltering earth.

At first Kabir is thrilled with every find, guessing how many tubers each plant will yield. He imagines himself an archaeologist and whoops with excitement when he spots the tiniest ones hidden like golden beads in the lumps of dirt. But soon he grows bored, and Aryan has to shout at him to stop him from playing with the puppies rather than sift through the clods he has overturned with the fork.

Aryan's back is stiff with always being bent to the earth the same way. The muscles in his neck complain when he turns to look over his shoulder. The digging fork is too big for his frame and every new swing tires him; his hands grow sore from pulling the dying plants from the soil. There are always more boxes to fill, always more rows to work.

He reckons that nearly five months have passed. He is impatient to be on their way.

On a new page in his notebook Aryan tries to work out some numbers.

In Istanbul, Ahmed told them that the smugglers were asking two thousand five hundred euros for a place in a truck that would go through Patras to Italy. Aryan has no idea how far they are from the Greek port, but calculates they would have to work five months to earn that much.

Aryan says nothing to Kabir. But he is starting to wonder if the farmer really is going to organize their ride.

'When are we going to England?' Kabir keeps saying.

The farmer cuts Aryan off mid-sentence when he asks.

'Look,' the farmer says, with a gesture that sweeps the hills.

Beyond the rise, the onion fields stretch before them, green leaves spiky as pencils that recede into a distant, knee-high wall.

It is night and Kabir can't sleep. The moon streams light into the room. Far away a dog is howling. Not-So-Old Dog answers from somewhere behind the house.

'Aryan?' he says.

'Mmmm.'

'Are you asleep?'

'Yes,' Aryan says.

'Then how come you're talking to me?'

'I'm not talking to you. I'm sleeping.'

A small silence.

'Aryan?'

'Mmmm.'

'Am I an Afghan?'

'Mmmm.'

'Am I?'

'Are you what?' Aryan clambers up through his tiredness.

'Am I an Afghan?'

'What do you mean, are you an Afghan?'

'Can you still be an Afghan if you can't remember anything about it?'

'Of course you're an Afghan. I'm an Afghan, you're an Afghan, our family is from Afghanistan.'

'But if someone asks, I can't tell them what it's like. I can remember more about Iran and Istanbul and this farm than Afghanistan.'

'That's because you were only four when we moved to Iran. What would you be if you weren't an Afghan?'

'I don't know. Maybe I'm not anything at all.'

'Of course you're an Afghan. Do you think you'd be here if you were an Egyptian or an American or an Eskimo?'

'OK, so tell me about Afghanistan,' Kabir says.

Aryan pauses. 'Can you remember the house?'

Kabir is silent for a moment. 'I can't see it in my head any more,' he says. In his voice there is something bordering on distress.

Aryan is fully awake now. 'Of course you can. You remember the pigeons that Grandpa used to look after, don't you? He used to take you up there sometimes, when you were still a yowling baby, so you could see the rooftops of the town.'

Kabir hesitates. 'I remember the white feathers and the pink claws, and their shiny, orange eyes. But I don't remember where it was. I can't even remember what Grandpa looked like.'

'He was very old. He had a wiry white beard and he had one funny leg. It used to take him ages to get up the stairs to the roof. His hands smelt of soap and he always wore a *pakol*,' Aryan says.

'I remember the *pakol*,' says Kabir. 'He used to put it on my head and it covered my eyes and prickled.'

'You see?' Aryan says. 'You do remember.'

'What else?'

'What about the bazaar where Baba used to go to buy pine nuts and pomegranates? You must remember that,' Aryan says. 'Madar used to go crazy when he took you. She yelled at him saying he'd put you down some place and you'd wander off and get lost. But you wanted to go on his shoulders, and you screamed so much if you couldn't go that he took you along just to stop your yelling. Surely you haven't forgotten that!'

Kabir wrinkles his nose, trying to summon the earliest pictures of his short life.

'And the TV, remember the old TV? There was no electricity so Baba linked it up with jump leads to a car battery under the table – there were all those wires – and it made a sound like hissing, and the picture looked like it was being beamed through a dust storm.'

'I remember the battery!' Kabir says, his face lightening. 'Yes, now I remember. The pincers on it were red and blue.'

'You see?' Aryan says. 'Even though you were only four you do remember.'

'So I am from Afghanistan,' Kabir says.

'Yes,' Aryan says. 'Now go to sleep like any normal Afghan.'

'But, Aryan?'

'Yes, Kabir.'

'I can't remember Baba any more.'

Aryan is caught offguard. He doesn't want to think about the last time he saw his father, the nightmare scenes with the spilled apples that creep up on him even when he is awake. He swallows, puts on his cheerful voice.

'He was very tall, so tall he laughed at you when you wanted to go anywhere with him because you only came up to his knees. He called you his grasshopper because you were forever leaping up to follow him around.'

Kabir says nothing. He has heard these stories before but Aryan knows he wants him to tell them again.

'He had big hands, and a scratchy face where he used to shave his beard till the Taliban came,' Aryan said. 'Then he grew a beard too, like all the men. It had colours in it that were different from his hair. When he'd been to the bazaar his clothes came back smelling of tobacco smoke. And he played chess better than anyone in the whole town.'

'I don't remember him playing.'

'He didn't play at home. He played in the bazaar after he lost his job when they burned down the school. They drank tea and smoked and played chess and he was always the best. That's why he tried to teach me.'

'Did you get good at it too?'

'He nearly always beat me. Sometimes I won – though maybe he just let me. He got cross when I missed the obvious moves and then he had no mercy, and punished me by wiping out all my men.'

'Can you teach me to play chess too?'

'You wouldn't like it. It's for grown-ups. There are lots of pieces and they all go different ways.'

'I forget faces but I'm good at remembering things like that.'

'When you are bigger and we find a board I'll show you the rules. Then I can use all Baba's tricks to give you a thrashing.'

'Not if I get better than you!'

'Well I haven't heard of any grasshoppers that can play chess, so you'll have a lot of catching up to do. Now be quiet and try to get some sleep.'

Aryan lies awake for a long time, thinking. It worries him that it is getting harder, whenever Kabir asks, to dredge up his own memories of their father. It is as if the definition of Baba's profile, in the dust-scratched photo in his wallet, is already fading, its power to evoke the scent of his father's skin, the rough feel of his hands, evaporating. Digging back through the past, clutching at stories that seem to ossify into something more lifeless with each retelling, is becoming more exhausting each time. Yet without the retelling, some vital thread will be broken; it is as if in reminding Kabir of their past he is also reminding himself, and in that way each becomes the keeper of the other's identity. Without Kabir, Aryan feels some part of him would cease to exist, and that his life before this journey would have no substance that even he could believe in. Sometimes he feels he could float off into space like an astronaut tethered neither by orbit nor gravity, and that he has such slim purchase upon the Earth that it would make no difference to anyone.

It is the end of the afternoon when an old truck pulls up covered in a green tarpaulin. Aryan is standing shirtless at the tap in the dying light of the day. There are rivulets of dirt down his arms and tiny moon craters in the dust.

Aryan hears the driver rip at the handbrake and swing himself out of the cabin and into the yard. The pigs grunt behind the rotting slats of their pen.

When Aryan looks up again the man is staring at him with the small, hard eyes of a lizard; his mouth is arranged in a strange half-smile. He doesn't turn away when Aryan sees him watching, but holds his gaze as if in expectation.

Something cold slithers down Aryan's spine. His mouth turns dry and his tongue feels thick inside it.

Kabir comes out of their sleeping place. He is looking for the stick he throws to the dogs. He stops when he sees the figure beside the truck.

The man gazes a moment longer, then turns and walks into the house.

'Who's that?' Kabir asks.

Aryan shrugs.

When the man comes outside again, he is arguing in Greek with the farmer. He strides across the yard, boots flinging small pieces of mud into the air, and flicks a half-smoked cigarette into the dirt; a thread of smoke unfurls like a small act of defiance. He swings himself back into the driver's seat. The wheels spin as he reverses past the gate.

Stony-faced, the farmer stands in the doorway, arms crossed, watching the truck disappear. He looks at the boys for a moment with an expression Aryan can't decipher, then goes inside.

It is first light, and the rows of onions beckon to them, rippling like a lake in the early summer breeze.

The farmer has given them wide, flat-pronged forks to dig around the bulbs. In the cool of the dawn he shows them how to pull them out carefully without damaging the skin, and then strip the dirt off with their hands. With a handheld scythe they lop off the leaves and fill the mesh sacks with brown balls.

'Small hands are good for this work,' the farmer says. 'This is a good job for you boys.'

Kabir squats close to the stalks, pulling them up with both hands and dusting them off. The puppies tangle between his feet. Sometimes he slaps them away.

The weather is getting hot. By the middle of the day they've peeled down to their T-shirts. They are sunburnt on their faces and necks and on their arms where their T-shirts end. They slap at mosquitoes and stinger wasps.

Crouched for hours in the same position, Aryan thinks his back is going to break. He also notices how the muscles in his arms are filling out and growing hard.

At noon they take a breather in the transparent shade of the olive trees. Small flies buzz around their faces, excited by the smell of sweat. The plastic bottles they refill for water are warm despite being buried up to their necks in the soil.

Men who arrived soon after them are working the nearby fields. They don't speak, but toil right through the hottest part of the day, turning each row into a knobbly ridge of red bags. A trail of discarded leaves floats behind them like a wake.

They must be paid by the sackful, Aryan thinks. That must be why they don't stop. He wonders where they go at night, and whether he and Kabir will be travelling with them when the farmer finally sends them on their way.

By the end of the day, all Aryan can think about is lying down. As soon as he is horizontal, he rolls off a precipice into sleep.

A conversation is taking place between their parents. They are in the house with the dovecote on the roof; the pigeons have filled the perches and the breeding boxes with their feathers and their warm beating hearts. Aryan is coming downstairs to get another blanket. It is early summer and he is sleeping outside, under the open sky, under the stars.

'If we don't leave he will end up just like them,' his father is saying.

Their mother is crying softly. She says she doesn't want to leave Afghanistan. She doesn't want to leave the house, nor the area around it where all her family are, nor the place where they buried Bashir. But Baba is telling her that soon they will have no choice.

There has been another rocket attack. Young men are being recruited. The commanders are again pressuring families for their sons.

'In the villages they are offering money to the fathers,' Baba is saying. 'They are taking boys as young as eleven and twelve.'

Aryan knows his father wants them to leave because of him. He has never been to Iran and doesn't want to go. There has been no school for months but he likes playing chess with Baba in the bazaar, and games of marbles with his friends in the dusty streets.

At the end of the day they sometimes see the old woman at the washing line. She never comes to talk to them, not even when she shuffles across the yard in her worn cloth shoes to bring them their food at night. She never smiles, her expression darkened by the map of lines and nodes on her face.

Aryan notices little things at first, and they are so small he doesn't know whether to believe it's a change at all.

First it is just a flicker of the curtain that makes him wonder whether the old woman has been watching them return from the fields.

Then there is the matter of the ice for his ankle, and the

ancient aspirin. And the salt-and-sugar water for Kabir when he was sick. And Aryan's hard-boiled egg.

One day Kabir goes to the house to ask for soap, and returns with an apricot in each hand.

At dusk, when they come in from the fields and the puppies are leaping all around, Kabir starts taking them to the house to be fed. The old woman tosses them some scraps from the table, and when he steps over the threshold, she lets him spend a few minutes inside.

When he comes back he tells Aryan about the big fire in the old wood stove in the kitchen, the blue china plates in the dresser, the different things she has stewing on the hob. Aryan can tell he misses having a home.

Sometimes the old woman asks him to peel apples, wash the fruit she intends to preserve, take potato peelings out to the pigs. They communicate through guesswork and gesture. In return she gives him food to share with Aryan – sometimes cheese and spinach pastries, small meat pies with peas.

Always she sends him away again before the farmer comes indoors.

Aryan isn't sure what to make of it. Sometimes he is glad for half an hour away from his little brother; he knows the old woman's company reminds Kabir of things Aryan steels himself against missing. But if Kabir is away too long, anxiety begins its slow ascent of his spine.

Once, beating the mud off his shoes, Aryan looks up to see the old woman in front of the curtain. With an arthritic hand she waves to him, just once, and disappears. Aryan pauses, then crosses the yard.

Inside, the old woman indicates he should wash his hands, and nods towards a chair. They sit around a sturdy wooden table peeling carrots and turnips and the potatoes they have dug from the fields. Aryan is surprised at the simplicity of the house that is not so different from some of those in the place where he was born.

The silence is filled with the bobbing of lids on the stove and the scrape of the peelers as they expose the strips of colour hidden under the vegetable skin.

Then the woman places a bowl of soup in front of them.

When the farmer comes inside he halts in the doorway, staring as Kabir slurps from the spoon. He says something angry in Greek but the woman cuts him off with words that ring out like slaps.

After that, they eat in the kitchen every day, leaving always before the farmer sits down with the old woman for his meal.

Sometimes when they return from the fields they find she has changed the blankets in their room, or put newspaper inside the window frames to stop the wind getting in.

Once, making their way back from the onion fields at dusk, they see the top of the truck with the green tarpaulin sway-ing down the corrugated driveway as it heads from the house towards the road.

The farmer, bent over a cracked ploughshare, ignores them as they walk past.

It is night when the shadows creep up on Aryan.

Bad dreams must have woken him initially, but it's the shivering that won't let him slip back under the blanket of sleep. It begins imperceptibly at first, like ripples in a glass of water, tugging him awake. But soon it builds, and Aryan knows with a sort of inevitability that it will not be stilled. His teeth chatter, and in time, his whole body shakes with it. Terrors he can't put any name to swirl like flying beasts with velvet bodies and whirring wings that brush against his face. Suddenly he is terrified of suffocation. His body has gone cold and not even the trembling of his limbs will restore his body heat. His mouth is dry and his face is suddenly bathed in sweat.

Through the window pane he can see only four black squares of night. The world is in darkness and from his pallet the hills block out the sight of any stars.

Aryan recognizes his demon fears; he starts to wonder whether they won't make the entire journey with him. For a while it seemed he had shrugged them off, that they had abandoned him in the shimmering desert, in the stony mountains of Kurdistan, in the hamlet where they were marooned for weeks, hiding from the soldiers while they waited for a guide. In the boat that barely made it across the waters of Lake Van, where fear of drowning lapped at the overwashed sides. There were other demons to displace them then – hunger, the pain of blistered heels and beaten shins, the smugglers who abandoned stragglers by the way. Perhaps they were jealous or just indolent demons; where the going was hardest they left him mercifully alone; there, he fell fitfully asleep, exhausted by the toil of advancing.

But as soon as they stop anywhere they catch up with him again; now, for the first time since Istanbul, the demons of immobility are back. They bore deep into his anxiety about all the days they are wasting; they undermine his resolve with doubt about the future; they gnaw at his strength of mind by rehearsing what it is they have fled.

Where are they heading really? He and Kabir could be stuck in this place for ever. He has heard stories of the missing who are never found, the rumours of body-organ harvesters, child enslavers and prostitution rings. Though things look peaceful here, and there is no war in Europe, he is suddenly aware of how easy it would be to disappear someone who no one knew existed in these lands.

He is ashamed to wish it, but suddenly he longs for his mother. He wishes he were as small as Kabir and could be enfolded in arms that would contain him, and calm him, and see the demons off into the wind.

He can't remember the scent of her any more, only that it was the same as her clothes.

When dawn comes, Aryan has not slept. He feels ragged and wrung out. The night lies heavy upon him, thick as dew.

The truck with the green tarpaulin starts coming by every second day, and parks on the shady side of the house. The driver talks to the farmer in Greek. Aryan sees his reptile eyes watching him over the top of their conversation. He fixes Aryan directly in his sights as he talks.

Aryan hasn't got used to seeing him. Even from a distance there is something that makes him recoil.

The man smokes with the farmer while Aryan and Kabir bundle the sacks of onions into the truck; some of them are nearly as tall as Kabir. Aryan shudders under the driver's stare, hoists the bags mechanically, hopes the tension in his stomach isn't legible on his face.

The days are hotter now. There is no shade in the fields where they work. At night they sleep fitfully, woken often by the drone of mosquitoes.

One day, the driver approaches them where the furrows extend close to the house. He feels and feels in his loose trouser pocket, and then extends a small packet.

'You smoke?' he says to Aryan in English.

Aryan doesn't respond.

With a smile and a fleshy hand the man proffers the half-crushed red-and-white packet, a cigarette protruding from the corner. 'Smoke like a man?' he says.

Aryan's eyes narrow. 'No,' he says.

The driver is standing very close to him now, and Aryan's mouth is dry. He can smell his odour of hair oil

and sweat; the skin on the back of his puffy hands is dry
and flaky and white.

The man hesitates a moment, shrugs, and goes back to
the truck. He doesn't even check the tarpaulin before
reversing out the gate. Aryan watches the top of the vehicle dip and sway over the potholes.

Two days later, at noon, he is there again. He talks with the
farmer while the boys load the morning's sacks into the
lorry. From the corner of his eye Aryan sees him climb into
the driver's seat.

'*Yassas!*' Aryan jumps when he hears the man's too-loud
voice. Kabir is dragging a sack towards the truck and the
man is blocking his path.

Two glass bottles of Coke glint in his dry, white hands.
He is holding one out to Kabir. 'Take,' he says. 'For you.'

Though the mornings still start off cool, the middle of
the day is hot and both of them are thirsty from the work.
Kabir reaches for the bottle.

'Leave it, Kabir!' Aryan says.

Kabir freezes in surprise. 'Why?' he says, hesitating, his
hand outstretched.

The man ignores Aryan and smiles at Kabir.

'Just don't!' Aryan catches himself shouting. His own
vehemence surprises him.

'There's one for you too,' Kabir says.

'I don't care – don't take anything from him.' Aryan
doesn't want them to accept any gift from this man. He

doesn't want to feel they owe him anything. He doesn't want them to feel the ties of obligation that gratitude inevitably brings.

Kabir takes the bottle. The man whips out a bottle opener and, placing his heavy hand on top of Kabir's, flips the cap off into the grass. His hand covers Kabir's entirely; he lets it linger there a long moment before taking it away.

'And you?' the man turns to Aryan.

Aryan stands rigid as stone.

The man waits for him to change his mind, then places the second bottle on the ground. He says something to them in Greek, smooths Kabir's hair and cheek, and climbs back into the truck.

Aryan's bottle stands alone among the green onion leaves, glistening, erect as a statuette.

There is a sound of wheels spinning on gravel as the truck pulls out into the road.

'Why did you take that bottle?' Aryan says.

'Why shouldn't I?' Kabir says. 'He just wanted to be nice.'

'I told you not to.'

'You're not my father.'

'That's right, Kabir, but I'm all you've got. And I'm telling you: keep away from that man.'

'Why should I?' Kabir says. 'At least he's nicer than you.'

'Just listen to me.' Aryan's voice is angry. 'He is not a good person.'

74

'What would you know?' Kabir is shouting back. 'He only wanted to give us a present.'

'You don't know the first thing about him.'

'Neither do you!'

'No,' Aryan said. 'But I'm older than you and I don't trust him.'

'Why do I always have to do what you say? You never want us to have any fun.'

'It's not about fun,' Aryan says.

'Well I'm keeping my bottle.'

'Do what you like then,' Aryan says.

'I will,' says Kabir. 'And I'm having yours too.'

Kabir snatches the lone bottle from the ground, shoves it in his pocket, and sits down some way from Aryan with his back to a fence post.

There are things Aryan can't tell Kabir. There are things Aryan can hardly bear to think about himself, but they are so indelibly inside him now that they have become part of the way he reacts before thought can intervene, part of the wounded place that was opened up inside him before he had the words or the knowledge to fight.

It had happened when they were still living in Afghanistan. There had been an older cousin who had shown an interest in him, taken him fishing on the lake in his taxi on the days when there was no school, taught him how to knot ropes and sharpen knives. Aryan had loved the sense of adventure, and the way it made him feel special, and the manly things he learnt that he could show off to the other boys.

But after a while his cousin stopped taking him straight home from their expeditions.

'I just have to pick something up here,' he'd say, turning off the rutted road. But there was never any house, and never anything to pick up.

In the beginning Aryan didn't understand what was happening. It felt strange at first that this burly man would sometimes paw his hair or his face, or put his big scratchy hands on his chest beneath his shirt. Aryan didn't like the feel of his skin or the smell of his animal sweat. But he had no words for what he was doing, or what it made him feel, and if he just ignored it, he thought the man would eventually lose interest. Instead, his explorations continued.

The first day he went too far, they had driven a long way from anywhere, and Aryan's cries and his seven-year-old's attempt to fight off a grown man had simply made his cousin laugh. But when Aryan managed to wriggle free, and took off across the land, the cousin roared after him and caught up with him and pinioned him and took off his belt and whipped him, and spat out at him that struggling would make things a lot worse.

To Aryan, what happened next was unspeakable, and had no name. He had never felt pain like it. The rocks digging into his ribs and the side of his face where the man was holding him down were nothing in comparison

76

to the tearing. But he also felt something give way in his heart. In the place where trust had been there came both shame and a sort of wordless fury; where he once felt sure of himself he felt mistaken, that he had somehow brought this upon himself, that in some major sense he had failed.

Afterwards, Aryan bled for a week every time he relieved his bowels. 'He slipped on the rocks by the lake,' his cousin had told his father to explain the bruising. If he breathed a word, his cousin had said, he would receive a belting that would make the last one seem like a tickle.

And so Aryan kept silent, and endured when avoidance failed. But he hated his cousin with the livid emotion of childhood, and was glad when the fighting made his whole family move away.

Two days later Aryan is stooped over the onion furrows, digging the papery brown spheres from the earth. They have reached the far end of the field, and are working close to a stone wall. He calls to Kabir to fetch more sacks.

It is a while before he realizes Kabir hasn't replied.

Aryan stands up and leans on his fork, stretching out his back. He looks around. Kabir is nowhere in sight. Nor is the truck that rolled up in the mid-afternoon.

Aryan hurries to the edge of the field, wondering if Kabir has wandered off to the latrine. 'Kabir!' he shouts. The warm air reverberates with his call, but no voice answers back.

Anxiety blinds him. Aryan leaps over the furrows to the wall, pushes himself over the top of it and tears into the next field. The farmer is wiring seedlings to stakes.

'Kabir, Kabir, where is he?' he says between gasps for breath.

The farmer looks at him sideways and straightens till his singlet stretches taut across his paunch.

'Who?' he says.

'My brother, Kabir.'

'He went with the driver to get more crates,' the farmer says. 'They'll be back soon.'

Aryan turns in a circle, scans the horizon, throws his open arms to his sides.

'Kabir,' he yells with all his lungs. The scarred and empty hillsides swallow his cry.

It is nearly nightfall before the truck returns.

Kabir is belted into the front seat. His face shimmers white through the windscreen. Tear stains streak his fat cheeks.

The driver greets the farmer with a cheery smile. 'Here's your working man back again,' he says. He starts to unload the empty crates.

Aryan is nauseous with anxiety and relief.

Kabir undoes the seatbelt and slides stiffly out of the truck. He cannot speak and there is no light in his eyes. He refuses to meet Aryan's gaze.

In their outhouse, Kabir turns his back to his brother and doesn't want to sleep anywhere near.

'Kabir,' Aryan says. 'Did he hurt you?'

Kabir is silent. But tears or the beginning of tears are smudging his charcoal eyes.

'Did the driver hurt you?' Aryan says.

Kabir says nothing.

'Come here,' Aryan says.

His brother doesn't move.

So Aryan goes to him and puts his arms around his brother's rigid frame. Kabir's whole body is trembling, and in that involuntary reaction, Aryan suddenly knows that his instincts were right.

Kabir doesn't turn to him when he speaks. 'Why didn't you tell me?' he says.

'I tried to warn you,' Aryan says. 'I didn't know for sure.'

'You didn't warn me. You just said not to take the bottle.'

'I had a bad feeling about him, that was all. I tried to make you listen.'

Kabir lets out a sob.

'He was too strong, Aryan.' Whatever else he is about to say is drowned out as the round shoulders heave.

Aryan looks at his brother, taking in as if for the first time how small he is, the ridges of his backbone under his grubby T-shirt, the baby down on his cheeks, the thick unruly hair.

He is so used to having him beside him that Aryan sometimes forgets he is still a child. A knot of misery rises

79

to his throat. He has failed to shield the one person left to him in the world to protect.

'Kabir,' he murmurs. 'It's not your fault.'

Kabir does not respond.

That is when Aryan decides. 'I don't care how we go. But we are not staying here any more,' he says.

Kabir takes a deep breath.

'What about the truck?' he says.

'I don't know whether there *is* any truck, Kabir. Maybe they never intended to send one. Maybe they never intended to pay.'

Aryan counts the days tallied in his notebook. Seven months. Apart from that one payment, there have been no wages and no onward journey. He feels weak at the thought of how much time they have lost. Soon he will be too old to go to school. He doesn't know how, yet, but they will be gone before what happened to Kabir can happen again. He is angry, like he was angry once before, and his anger will carry them out like a lifeboat.

The farmer is fixing a fence on the far side of the land. The driver with the fleshy hands hasn't shown up this time; a younger man has driven the truck in his stead.

Aryan sends Kabir into the truck and passes the sacks and crates of onions up to him, one by one. When the last one is loaded he clambers aboard, then rearranges them to make a space, like the dens he and Zohra used to build with rugs and cushions and the table in the house in Afghanistan.

'Make yourself small,' he tells Kabir. 'Don't make a sound.'

He pushes his brother into the gap and crouches low beside him in the niche. In his pocket he has two heels of bread that he has saved from the last two mornings.

The driver pulls the canvas taut and tightens the ropes without seeing them. The engine revs. He honks his horn once to let the farmer know he is on his way.

'*Yassas!*' the farmer shouts back from the field.

It is almost too easy. Aryan has no idea where the truck is going, but at least they are on the move. Kabir looks like he is under water in the green tarpaulin light.

'Will the puppies be all right?' Kabir whispers.

Aryan feels a pang. But they could not have taken them.

'They've still got Not-So-Old Dog to protect them,' he says.

The sky is the deepest blue and the streetlights are still on when Aryan peers through the gap he has opened in the canvas. The truck has stopped at a service station; he is assailed by the odour of petrol that always made him feel queasy, even when he has had enough to eat.

The driver slams the cabin door. Aryan waits a moment, then takes a chisel he has found in the truck and tears a slit in the tarpaulin. Sliding the crates apart, he looks out. All he can see is the bitumen of a car park and the wall of another truck.

'Let's go,' he tells Kabir. He pushes his brother through the opening, then slithers down beside him, favouring his strong ankle. His vertebrae scrape on the truck's metal ridge as he drops.

On creaking legs they stumble into a salt-sticky dawn. From the sound of seagulls he guesses they are near a rubbish dump, or somewhere along the coast. They hover between the semi-trailers, and duck under the wheels of one to wait till their driver returns. He starts the engine and pulls back on to the highway; they watch till the green tarpaulin is eclipsed by the traffic.

There is no soap or paper towels in the men's restroom and the water is cold.

Side by side they piss into a reeking urinal. Aryan steps over the leaking floor and uproots two handfuls of paper from a cubicle. They wash their faces and dry them off and look at themselves like startled strangers in the spotted mirror.

'Where is this place?' Kabir says.

'I think we're still in Greece. At least all the number plates are Greek.'

He flattens his brother's springy hair with water and straightens his clothes.

'We have to try not to look too obvious,' Aryan says.

'I'm hungry,' Kabir says. Aryan ignores him and the dragging emptiness of his own stomach.

Aeroplanes cruise low overhead, landing gear extended like talons. From the airport, Aryan thinks, there must be transport into a city.

'You got your marching shoes on?'

Kabir nods.

Aryan is worried by how quiet he has become. He hopes that every kilometre he puts between them and the farm will help him forget.

'We'll get something to eat in the city, don't worry,' he tells Kabir.

Around them the land is bald. Treeless mountains brood at the far edge of a flat industrial plain that is spliced by freeways. They skirt the back of the petrol station and walk along a road that merges up ahead with a highway. A railway line divides its two arteries of traffic; a train ambles into a deserted platform.

Aryan grabs Kabir by the hand. They clamber on to the motorway shoulder. 'Ready?' he says, searching for a break in the traffic.

At the first gap between the vehicles they run. There is a wailing of horns as cars and trucks speed by in a surge of wind. Aryan's heart pounds as they clamber over the road divider and flatten themselves against the waist-high metal barrier. Whistling vehicles whip their hair into their eyes and tear at their clothes in both directions now. Shapes like metallic walls roar by so fast that their colours bleed; the world is streaked with sound and light and the rush of exhaust-laden air. Kabir slips but steadies himself on the barrier.

'Ready?' Aryan shouts again above the roaring. His brother is leaning backwards like a man unhinged. The vehicles thin out momentarily, and they hurl themselves across the tide.

Another blasting of horns, but they're across.

They jump over a concrete wall and land on a sandy path that runs beside the railway tracks. Ahead, a few low steps lead up to the platform. On one side of it hangs a blue sign with a picture of an aeroplane. On the other, the word 'Athina'.

They pause for a moment, catching their breath. Kabir rolls up his trouser leg; his shin is bleeding where he has skinned it on the barricade.

'We'd better get a ticket,' Aryan says. A staircase to the ticket office soars over their heads.

At the window Aryan pulls out a twenty-euro note.

'Two,' he says.

A young woman, black hair streaked blonde, says something at high velocity they don't understand. 'Airport, or Athens?' she repeats in impatient English through a gap in the glass.

'Athens,' he says. With relief, he recognizes the name.

Speaker-buds in her ears, she barely looks at them as she taps a machine with fingernails ornamented with intricate flowers. Kabir can just see over the counter; he squints to watch the miniature decorations rise and fall as she works.

Bored, the woman slaps two tickets from a wooden holder on to the counter. She slides their change under the glass without a glance.

Copying a young man in front of them, they feed their tickets into a greedy turnstile that spits them out again with a whirr of mechanical disdain.

Back on the platform, they sit cross-legged on the sun-warmed concrete to wait. They pitch pieces of gravel at a discoloured soft-drink can discarded on the far side of the rails.

They get off with the tourists from the airport at a station before the end of the line. The train has left the lighted world behind and burrowed deep underground; the platform is aswirl with people.

Aryan stands aside to let the tourists wheel their oversized suitcases past. In the dimness and the crush he has lost his bearings; the weight of earth and concrete oppress him; he just wants to go onwards, or up.

In the carriage he has shown Kabir the piece of paper where Ahmed wrote 'Victoria Park'. There were pictures of a ship and a temple and the Olympic rings on the diagram above the doors, but no sign of any parks. On the platform he cannot decipher the maps in frames on the walls.

He stops an old man in too-long shoes clutching the arm of his wife. A transparent pyramid of plastic dangles from her finger; Kabir peers at the biscuits arranged inside.

They argue, they point and gesticulate, but Aryan cannot make out their Greek.

All bra straps and flashing jewellery, a woman clatters past too hurried to notice Aryan's appeal. A man with a white cane tap-taps along the platform as if sweeping it for mines. Finally they intercept a young man who looks like a student, with holes in his jeans and hair glued into a miraculous point.

'There is no Victoria Park in Athens,' the student says, when at last he understands where they want to go.

Ahmed had been so definite. Aryan insists.

'There is Victoria metro station and that is not far from a big park in Alexandras Street,' the student says. 'Maybe that's the one you want.'

Aryan hesitates. Maybe he is right. If there is no Victoria Park, perhaps Ahmed meant the park that's near the station.

'Yes,' Aryan says. 'I think it's OK.'

The student leads them up escalators and through passageways of gleaming stone.

Kabir gazes with amazement at the moving staircases. He pauses a second before jumping on, loses his balance, and steadies himself on the handrail that goes at a different speed from the stairs.

'Two stops only,' the student says, illustrating the information with his fingers when they reach the platform. 'Omonia, Victoria. There you get out. The park is very close. Just ask for a street called Alexandras if you get lost.'

He makes Aryan repeat the name.

Aryan touches his heart and shakes his hand, and Kabir solemnly follows suit. The student is surprised, then smiles. In moments he is enclosed by the crowd; it is like he never existed, or did so, ephemeral as a firefly, only to light their way.

Almost immediately they run into a group of Afghans sitting under the trees. They are Hazaras from the south. One of them leads Aryan and Kabir across the park and through the streets to a hotel where the rooms are €3.50 a night.

'You need a travel agent?' asks the man behind the desk. Aryan stares at the shiny scar that links his right nostril to his eye.

He hadn't imagined it would be so simple.

They take a room for one night. Kabir drags his feet up the interminable staircase, pushing himself from wall to wall. The number on the key leads them to a room, little bigger than the two narrow beds inside it, pungent with stale cigarettes. There is one small window almost at the level of the ceiling. Aryan works its wooden shutter open by pulling on a dirty string; the light it lets in is grey, reflected off an outside wall.

The twin beds sag even before they collapse on to chenille bedspreads rubbed thin by the countless bodies that have lain there before them.

Aryan pulls from his inside pocket the pieces of bread

that he has saved from the farm, and hands one to Kabir. The crusts are so hard their gums bleed.

Later, Aryan shows Kabir how to work the shower, and waits for him in the room. When he comes back, pink-skinned and dripping-haired, Aryan takes his turn.

Aryan stands under the running water a long time. The tiles are cracked, and some are missing, and when he turns the hot tap a rusted pipe swings out from the wall. Brown veins marble a decaying cake of soap. But the lukewarm water washes the dust from his hair, prises the stiffness from his shoulders, and slowly eases the tiredness from his mind.

Pictures flash up and disintegrate like slides on a crumbling wall – the puppies batting potatoes between Kabir's feet; the old woman feeding them in silence at the kitchen table; Kabir's face in the dashboard light when the truck driver brought him back to the farm. He remembers the smell of earth under the truck's tarpaulin and Kabir awash in the aquarium light, and the student with the pointy hair who helped them in the metro. He lets his thoughts run with the water until it starts to turn cold and washes them down the half-choked drain.

Flowers of rust decorate the mirror that is covered in fog. Aryan traces a line across it with his finger and watches the drips race to descend. He dries himself with the scratchy towel that is too meagre to wrap around his hips, and pulls his dirty clothes back on. For the first time in months his body feels almost relaxed.

He pads back to their room along the tiled corridor and pushes open the door.

The room is empty.

Aryan seizes the key, slams the door behind him and flings himself down the staircase three steps at once. He slips on the foot-polished surface; manages to clutch the banister just in time. His heart slams against his ribcage like a drowning man.

Between gasps for air he tries to calculate how many minutes have passed, how far a small boy could have gone.

There is no one in the foyer; even the scar-faced receptionist has disappeared.

In the street he looks left and right, blinking in the glare, scanning the known world for a sign. Where, he thinks, where? The road is choked with traffic; his view is blocked by a stream of yellow taxis and white-windowed delivery vans. The sick feeling he remembers from the last time they were separated overwhelms him. The only place he can imagine is the park; panicked, he retraces their steps.

And then he sees him, sitting on a bench between the trees. He is watching a gang of children chase a football, a black-and-white dog yapping at their heels. In the glaring sunshine, Kabir looks forlorn.

Aryan leans forward, hands on his knees, to catch his breath. He can feel his heart pounding through the wash of relief.

He sinks beside his brother on the bench. It is a while

before he can talk; his mouth is sour with the aftertaste of panic.

'Don't do that,' Aryan says after a while.

'I only went for a walk.'

'I thought I'd lost you again.'

The first agent they meet looks scarcely older than Aryan. He has slicked-back hair and a nervous tic and mobile phones he juggles in each hand. He promises to get them to Italy for two thousand eight hundred euros.

Two thousand eight hundred euros, Aryan thinks. The number makes him feel weak. That is not the price they had calculated back in Iran, when he had discussed the cost of the journey, including bribes and agents' fees, with a man his uncle knew who had made it as far as Austria before getting sent back.

'Beware of the kidnap places inside Iran,' the man had said. 'Beware of the hostage takers who will beat you and imprison you until your relatives send more money. Beware of the intermediaries along the way, the heroin addicts and the small-town profiteers who will try to make you pay a second time for things already included in the price. And above all, beware of the smugglers. Your life is in their hands – remember to never, ever look them in the eye.'

The receptionist sets up a meeting with another agent. Aryan kicks Kabir under the counter; he cannot stop staring at the man's scar.

A six-foot Kurd, the agent looks more like a warrior

than a smuggler. He reminds Aryan of the gun-swinging horsemen who led them, on foot, over the mountains into Turkey, toting drugs with their barrels of oil. The man leers when he speaks and proposes a deal that Aryan instinctively mistrusts: two thousand nine hundred euros to guarantee their arrival in Rome.

When a third one sets the same price, tapping the figure into his calculator with a carpet seller's practised panache, Aryan tells the man it's too much. He hasn't got any solutions, but they will find some other way.

'How much have you got then?' says the man. A long-toothed Pakistani, he looks like a door-to-door salesman. A pod of cellphones nestle in the purple satin pockets of his briefcase.

Aryan has learned not to give any numbers away. 'Not as much as you're asking,' he says. He resists the urge to pat the side of his belt.

The salesman is undeterred. 'I will send you my colleague,' he says. 'He has a cheaper way.'

A young Pakistani with different-coloured eyes meets them in a metro station with a map. He stands with his back to the wall, on the lookout for any policemen on patrol.

'We go here, to this town, and this is where you get on the truck. This truck will take you to Italy.'

'Through Patras,' Aryan says.

'Not through Patras,' the man says. 'Inland. Fewer controls that way.'

'It looks very far by road,' Aryan says, looking at the red line of the highway, the backlands in green, the light-blue sweep of coast.

'For you it is better. It is safer,' the young man says. Aryan is unnerved by the way his blue eye seems larger than the brown. 'Out of sight of the police.'

Aryan looks at Kabir and hesitates.

'I can do a special deal for you, since your brother is small. We take many families this way. It is less because we can put more people on board.'

'How many people are you taking?' Aryan asks.

'A maximum of sixteen. I have two places left so I will do you a special offer, just one thousand two hundred euros for the two of you. One thousand two hundred is a very good price.'

Aryan reflects. 'When would we go?' he says.

'When the families are ready we will go. It's a matter of a couple of days.'

Aryan tells him he will think about it overnight.

'Don't take too long,' the smuggler says. He introduces himself as Ardi, but Aryan knows it's a false name. 'You're not the only ones wanting to go.'

'Tomorrow I will tell the receptionist,' Aryan says. 'He will let you know.'

Aryan still has one thousand four hundred euros sewn into the lining of his belt. If they use one thousand two hundred euros to get to Italy, that will leave only three hundred and forty-six euros to get them from Italy to England if he includes the money they got on the farm. It won't be enough. But at least they will be closer to their goal.

In the morning he asks the receptionist to tell Ardi they accept.

A week goes by before Ardi comes to find them in their new sleeping place, with a group of Afghan boys in Attiki Park.

The morning heat was already stifling when Aryan had met them, rummaging among the T-shirts in a street market that barrelled through a tunnel of trees. In the lime-green shade of the branches that wove into a cathedral overhead, Kabir had marvelled at the chandeliers of grapes, and the gargoyle faces of the curly-tailed fish.

'You can stay with us,' one of the boys had said when he realized Aryan and Kabir had just arrived. 'You can come with us when we go to the church for food.'

Watermelons were piled in precarious pyramids on the ground. Aryan's stomach churned as they went past.

Though the boys are kind, Aryan is impatient to leave. He is scared of the police, scared of the boys' tales, scared of getting stuck again when they have already lost so much time.

'Tomorrow morning, early, we go,' Ardi says. 'You will meet me by the metro station at six.'

Ardi sits several rows behind them in the bus and doesn't address them a single word.

They had hung back as he lined up at one of the windows of the low-roofed bus station, its destinations pressed in blue letters against the glass. Overhead, a pair of unsynchronized fans made half-hearted revolutions in the heat. Old ladies in black perched at plastic tables while the younger women, with prams and revealing tops, bought gnarled cheese rolls and fluorescent drinks for their kids. Busmen and taxi drivers embroidered the blinding day with tobacco smoke.

When Ardi was done, they followed him outside. He handed over their tickets with instructions: not to speak to him or show any sign they recognized him once they boarded the bus; to follow him at a distance when he got off.

Aryan had given him a third of the money and left the rest with the receptionist with the shiny scar. When they reached Italy he would call the hotel and tell the man to give Ardi the remainder.

The sun beats down on the side of the bus and the overhead air vents don't work. Kabir pulls the orange curtain across the window and leans against it, drowsy with heat. Amid the wasps and the mosquitoes and the cicadas they have slept badly in the park, but Aryan forces himself to stay awake, watching for when Ardi gets off.

Kabir's thick lashes look like feathers when his eyelids are shut, Aryan thinks; they cast shadows on his cheek where the sunlight filters through the curtain. Tenderness clutches his heart like a rabbit trap.

He stares at the sun-bleached landscape. The endless road reminds him of another journey, the last trip they made with their mother, on a dusty bus back to Afghanistan. He hadn't wanted to leave Afghanistan in the first place, but Baba was worried about the commanders; when he was killed they no longer had any choice. Then, after four years at school in Iran, Aryan hadn't wanted to return. But the UN had said it was safe, and Madar was missing her family, and they couldn't keep living in the tiny apartment with their cousins – even with Madar washing clothes all day and Aryan sewing in the afternoons with the tailor.

He remembers how happy Madar was to be going home. Her tired face was smiling for the first time in months as she packed their things and brushed Kabir's hair and put on what she called her sensible shoes. He couldn't have guessed that one month later she would be dead, that through his grief and anger he would have to sell every-thing, her gold jewellery and the silk carpets and the house, and take the dangerous route with Kabir all the way back to Iran, and bring him on the journey they were now on.

They stop at a roadside café selling bags of pistachio nuts and industrial cakes displayed behind finger-smeared glass. Irradiated purple, flies fizz and drop inside a fluores-cent grill. Two men with seafarers' faces play backgammon in a corner by the window, the counters click-clicking as they fly under quick-moving hands.

Ardi smokes a cigarette outside and doesn't even acknowledge them with a look.

It is several hours before they arrive in the town. They follow Ardi to the back of a truck that is parked on a quiet road.

They waste no time. Aryan gives Kabir a leg-up, and takes a last glance at the late-afternoon sky before he too slithers inside, slipping between the cartons that disguise a false wall.

Ardi presses himself against the boxes to let them pass. He speaks rapidly. 'You don't move, you are silent, you wait. You make no attempt to get off – you do that only when the driver decides.'

The truck sways slightly as he jumps off and slams the doors.

Aryan feels like a cave-dweller in the darkness. He waits for his eyes to adjust, but nothing happens. He switches on his mobile phone and its small green rectangle glows like the end of a tunnel.

With a start he realizes that the compartment is packed with people. There is a family from Bangladesh – a man and a woman, two children and a baby – some Iranian Kurds, and at least six other Afghans. They may be twenty-four people in all, arranged opposite each other, legs outstretched like a railway. The confined space is already warm and pungent with human sweat.

Aryan feels his heart sink. No wonder the price was

cheap: there are too many people inside, and they have no guarantee of success. The children, the baby with its cries, are sure to give them away.

'It's stifling in here,' Kabir says.

In the blackness, Aryan places his palm on Kabir's forehead. He can't tell if Kabir has a temperature or whether it's his own hot hand.

Aryan swallows. He feels his claustrophobia mounting, tries to bat away the terror of suffocation prickling at his throat. He concentrates on the truck's ceiling, imagines it soaring above them in the darkness, and outside, the arch of blue sky. His Turkish cellphone is slippery in his hand. He clutches it like a lifeline, checking the emergency numbers he has recorded there for both Italy and Greece after he talked with the men in the park, and the receptionist sold him a new card.

Someone hisses at him. 'Make sure that thing's turned off.'

The green rectangle shrinks and disappears.

In his other hand Aryan has the litre-bottle of water he bought when they got off the bus.

'You mustn't drink,' someone says in English, eyes better accustomed than his are to the dark. 'If you pee in the truck when we're on the ferry, you'll give us all away.'

'I didn't think we were going on the ferry,' Aryan says.

'What did you think this was, an aeroplane?'

'We *are* going to Italy?' Aryan says, suddenly worried Ardi has put them on the wrong truck.

'Sure,' comes the voice, scratchy and dry. 'At least that's the plan.'

'They told us we weren't going through Patras,' Aryan says.

'Well how did you think we were going to get there?' the scratchy voice says.

Aryan takes that in. Through the port, then, he thinks. He wonders how long it will take, and where they are going to end up.

'Don't worry about the water bottle,' he says. 'We have an empty one too.'

Someone grumbles about the baby. 'One cry out of him and we're done for,' the voice says.

Perhaps the mother has drugged it. It is sleeping soundly, making no noise.

Behind them, inside the truck, someone is sliding more packing crates against the compartment wall.

Gravel crunches and scatters, and the vehicle lurches on to the road.

It is hot in the truck and gradually even the whispering peters out.

In the gap opened up by the silence, Aryan finds himself thinking about Bashir.

He is not sure what has made him suddenly remember the brother whose presence he recalls more clearly than his face. Maybe it is the darkness in the truck, the way that no matter how hard he stares, how widely he stretches his eyes, he cannot even see his own hands. But suddenly Bashir is there in his mind, the gentle brother who was good at fixing things, and the picture of him the last time he saw him, his body dumped beside the graveyard without any eyes.

Though he was small he clearly remembers the day the Taliban came. There were insects crucified in the radiators of the four-wheel-drive Toyotas that pulled up in the street outside the house, and the entrails of a video tape trampled in the dirt beside the wheels. He remembers the men's dark turbans, and their car-antennae whips, and them asking for Ali and taking Bashir when Ali was nowhere to be found.

He remembers Baba's desperation, how he went first to the mullah, then to the jail and pleaded, how Madar went with her sister and begged, and their telling Baba they would give back Bashir only when he brought them Ali.

Nothing Baba told them made any difference: that they'd disowned Ali; that Ali had fled; that he wasn't part of the family any more. Still they kept him, until the day the neighbours came to tell them that they'd seen Bashir's fifteen-year-old body lying by the cemetery gate.

He remembers the day they buried him, the sound of his mother's wailing that bored deep into his chest, the way the light went out from Baba's eyes.

And he remembers the night a few weeks later when Ali crept home to tell them he was going to Pakistan. His face was dark and his eyes were hollow like he'd forgotten the very meaning of sleep. There were low males voices murmuring, the men of the family conferring. They said it didn't matter that the Taliban were wrong, that Ali had had nothing to do with the foreigners; if they believed he did then it was perilous for him to come home, and perilous for anyone to shelter him.

Madar couldn't stop crying when she saw Ali and hugged him till they thought he would break. Being pregnant with Kabir was no comfort for losing Bashir, and now she was losing another son.

That same night he left, and they never heard from him again.

Aryan doesn't look at the photo very often. But sometimes, when he pulls it out of his wallet, he wonders whether Ali is still alive; whether he knows that Baba was killed; whether he knows that they went to live in Iran. He wonders if he knows that Madar died when a car bomb exploded a month after they arrived back in Afghanistan.

Mostly Aryan is sure that Ali is dead. But sometimes he likes to imagine that he made it to Pakistan, and is living somewhere safe, and that one day he will hear about them and track them down to wherever they'll be living in England.

The truck deposits them on a roadside in the middle of nowhere before dawn.

'OUTOUTOUT!' the driver yells. He hits the nearest of them with a wheel wrench to make sure.

Spitting stones, the truck accelerates immediately into the fading night.

They stagger into the roadway, and break up into groups, and scatter in all directions. They are hunger-cramped, disoriented, cold. The baby, Aryan realizes, never once let out a cry.

Fleetingly, he wonders what will become of them, where each of them will go.

He and Kabir set off across a field, leaving a trail of footprints in the dew. There is the suggestion of sunrise beyond the mountains and a pale mist curtains the land. Like sleepwalkers they advance through the milky light, keeping parallel to a side track, detouring to steer clear of a farmhouse. They stay inside the fences and off the road.

Beyond a hill there is a crossroads. They follow the direction of the heaviest traffic. Aryan guesses it is heading towards a town.

'Wait here,' Aryan says. He heads down the slope towards a sign on the edge of the road.

He returns, kicking up clods of grass. He squints as the sun lifts over the hills. 'Genova,' he says to his brother's blurry outline.

'Where's that?'

Aryan shrugs. Then he turns on his mobile phone. After a moment the letters 'TIM' appear on his screen. He shows it to Kabir.

'Italy,' he says.

By the time they reach the centre, the city is awake. The streets get narrower and narrower until no car, no shaft of sunlight, can penetrate; even the rain, Aryan thinks, would have trouble getting in. There is so much stone encasing the earth that there are no cracks left for even the thinnest blade of grass. They wander, subdued, between the imposing buildings that nearly touch overhead as if striving to seal off the sky. Some are joined by vertiginous bridges that make Aryan think of tightrope walkers; his knees feel watery when he imagines what it would be like to go across.

There are antique shops with gold-edged furniture and tarnished chandeliers in the windows, and workshops where armchairs are having their stuffing put back in, and sweet shops with small white stones the shape of flattened eggs.

Other buildings, hewn from blocks of stone, loom as impenetrable as jails. They have brass rings on the outside as if ready to be towed away, or moored in case of floods. Squeezed beneath them are bars so narrow they have no room for any chairs; the aroma of coffee assaults them as they pass the open doors.

They come to a stripy church whose black-and-white stonework is repeated on the buildings around it, so that the whole square looks like it was decorated by a painter who didn't know when to stop.

Bent almost double, an old man is filling a plastic bottle at a stone fountain. When the bottle bubbles over he extracts a lid from his pocket and, with trembling hands, screws it into place. Slowly he reaches between his feet and fills another, but fumbles and drops the pink top, which peels away down the sloping cobbles in a hiccuping curve. Aryan darts after it and hands it back to the old man, who blinks myopic thanks. When he has sealed the second bottle the old man still doesn't straighten up, but shuffles off stuck in his right-angle, eyebrows raised over rheumy eyes as he peers into the day.

When he has gone, they lean their mouths into the fountain's blackened spout. They shiver as the icy water traces the map of their insides.

Suddenly they burst into sunlight. Where the old town spills on to the seafront they find themselves on the edge of a freeway; they can hear traffic speeding by on an over-pass above their heads. There is a car park, and a paved waterfront, and the carved prow of an old wooden ship that looks like it has sailed out of a legend.

On two long lines of sheets, African men are planting handbags and wooden figurines the way Afghan women set out tomatoes to dry in the sun. Aryan has never seen faces so black; Kabir hangs back, fascinated and a little scared.

Aryan approaches one of the men. He is plumping up his handbags with bubble-wrap and arranging them beside a menagerie of wooden frogs; strings of beads drape in thick lianas over his forearms.

'Can you tell me how to go to Rome?' Aryan says.

The man looks down at them. He has the whitest teeth Aryan has ever seen, and bloodshot eyes, and a leather thong of red, yellow and green beads around his neck.

The man calls over to another in a red baseball cap. 'Suleymane! Come here and tell me what these kids are saying.'

Aryan feels suddenly uneasy. The men are lean and tower over them. Others desert their wares to listen.

'Rome, can you tell us how to go to Rome?' Aryan says. He hopes the men don't notice the break in his voice.

'Rome is very far away, especially if you are going on foot,' the man in the baseball cap says with a laugh. 'Where are you from?'

'Afghanistan,' Aryan says.

He whistles, and Aryan hears the men pass the word around among them, the four-syllable name rolling off pink tongues.

'And where are you going?' he says.

'England.'

'Then Rome is the wrong direction,' the man says. 'You've already passed it.'

'I have to see my friend, one Afghan man, and he is there,' Aryan says. He clings to the address Ahmed gave them. He only trusts capital cities, the litany of stepping-stones he has forced Kabir to learn, the string of names that ensured they wouldn't get lost.

'Then you will have to take the train,' the man says.

'But be careful, there are many police about. If you like I can take you to the station.'

Aryan doesn't know whether to trust him. But in this town they have nowhere to go and no one else to ask.

'OK,' he says.

'Do you have money for the ticket?' the man asks.

'Yes.' Aryan fingers the two twenty-euro bills in his pocket.

'How much have you got?' the man says.

Aryan produces the notes he has folded into blue, origami squares; they stretch like waking butterflies unwrapping their wings in his palm.

The man plucks them from Aryan's hand, flattens out the creases, and slides them into a plastic wallet.

'Don't you worry, man, your money is safe with me,' he says.

Aryan's mouth feels dry; it has already forgotten the water of the old man's fountain.

The man tells them he will get their tickets. 'The night train is cheapest,' he says.

Aryan wants his money back. But he feels he cannot ask for it now.

'My name is Solomon, like the king,' the man says with a smile, extending an empty hand.

From the outside the station is a pink cake with frosting, balanced on a jumble of pillars and arcades. Aryan and Kabir follow Solomon inside. Its steep steps and brass balustrades feel sinister in the artificial light.

'Wait here,' Solomon says. He leaves them outside a shuttered newspaper kiosk and disappears.

Five minutes later he returns. 'It's OK,' he says. 'The train leaves just before midnight.'

Kabir is stumbling with tiredness. Aryan is relieved they will soon be on their way.

Solomon stands with them on the platform watching the train lumber in. The windows are opaque with the dirt of European cities; graffiti Aryan cannot read has been etched into the dust on its sides. Some of the cars are in darkness. They hurry along the platform until they find an illuminated carriage full of compartments that look like private rooms, with people sitting upright under luggage suspended overhead. The blinds on most of them are drawn but Solomon chooses one anyway and slides open the door. They are greeted by the scowls of an old lady in black and the snores of a man whose grey-stubbled jowl is compressed against the window. The tide of his breathing advances and recedes on the mirror of the glass. The air is ripe with the smell of salami and tinkles with the whisper of music. It emanates from a set of earphones being shared by a teenage couple, their heads resting together in a nest of hair. Aryan and Kabir sit side by side on the two empty seats that face the wrong way down the track.

'Have a nice journey,' Solomon says, shaking their hands.

He is gone before Aryan realizes that he has forgotten to give them their tickets.

Aryan jumps to the corridor window but it is cemented shut with grime. He presses his cheek to the glass as the train starts to move, but the red cap is nowhere in sight.

It is only later, when Kabir has passed out and the train is swaying and grinding through the darkness, through tunnels and along highways and past the back lots of dimly lit towns, that it dawns on him, through the hunger cramps in his belly and his exhaustion, that Solomon never even paid their fares.

Everyone in the carriage is dozing or asleep; Aryan imagines that he and the driver are the only people awake in the whole train. Kabir has found a blue plastic soldier buried in the crease between the seats and clutches it in his moist hand. He has curled up on the hard green vinyl and put his head on Aryan's lap. Aryan is tired too, but sleep won't come; he is angry about Solomon and their money, and worried about what lies ahead, and how they will find the people at the address in Rome. But there is also something about the inevitability of the train, as it rocks and sways and draws the future closer, that brings him a semblance of calm.

He rests his head against the glass of the compartment wall, and looks into its reflection. As he explores the reverse world he is suddenly aware that a pair of eyes is staring at him – the young girl with the headphones, her head on her boyfriend's shoulder. Aryan feels himself flush and looks away, wondering how long she has been watching him. But then he lets his gaze drift slowly up-up-up towards the luggage rack and down-down-down towards where she is sitting. Her eyes are closed again; she is breathing softly; she has fallen back to sleep.

Aryan can't help looking at her, at the moulded shape of her breast, the honey-coloured skin that disappears into the curve of her T-shirt. Her jeans are cut low, exposing a small sapphire in her navel. He is fascinated. It reminds him of the pictures of belly dancers pinned up outside restaurants that they giggled at in the streets of Istanbul; he couldn't fathom the attraction of their corpulence. But this girl is nothing like them.

The Afghan girls he knew would be shocked to see how women in Europe dressed out in the street, but to Aryan the sapphire is intriguing. He imagines the softness of the skin it nestles in, the fold of flesh against the cold, hard stone. His gaze moves up to her face. Her eyes are iridescent with eye-shadow that has smudged beyond their almond corners, and the colour of her lips reminds him of the poppy fields back home. He is entranced. He stares and looks away and stares again, nervous that the weight of his gaze might rouse her. He drags his eyes back to the glass where he can watch her reflection instead. Suddenly, in its mirroring surface against the blackness of the tunnels and the flickering night, he sees that her eyes are open, looking at him again. Something flutters in his stomach and he averts his gaze, hoping she hasn't noticed his stare. But, little by little, his eyes return to the glass. With disappointment and relief he sees that her reflected self is looking out the other window, and then she shuts her eyes again, drowsily, exposing the iridescent lids.

This time, Aryan allows himself to take everything in. His eyes follow the nape of her neck and the line of her cheek and the chestnut hair that falls over her boyfriend's shoulder. He traces the indent of her waist and the slight mound of her belly and the shape of her calf where it leans against her boyfriend's leg. The timpani pulse of the earphones has stopped, though the earbuds are still in place; perhaps they have run out of songs. He wonders how they met, what he did to charm her, what words he used to persuade her to be with him. In Afghanistan he would be able to think of something to say, but here? He sees the girl's chest move gently with her breathing, the curve of her breast like the soft swollen chest of a bird, and feels a pang of jealousy, and wishes the boy were anywhere but here.

He thinks of his cousin Zohra, and the Afghan girls he knew at home and in Iran – ardent, but kept in check by the consequences of allowing a boy too near. He lets his mind wander, lulled by the train and mesmerized by the girl's shape beneath the close-fitting clothes, by the sapphire and the symmetry of her reflection in the glass, until suddenly she opens her eyes. She sees Aryan looking at her reflected self and, catching his gaze in the glass, neither blinks nor turns away. Aryan swallows and feels he will faint and holds her stare, mortified at the stirring he tries to hide, trying to find the courage to turn and look at her in person. Finally, he manages it. And in that same instant she closes down again, shutting him out, so all he can see is the movement of her eyeballs like small marbles beneath their peacock-feather lids.

It takes them some time to find the place.

The train arrives in Rome at dawn and no one stops them or asks for their tickets as they find their way out of the station. They weave through the rush-hour throng, intoxicated by the scent of aftershave and pollution. They watch trams rounding cobbled corners snapping with electricity. They stare at short-skirted women on motor-scooters pausing at the traffic lights in helmets and spindly high-heels.

In the narrow streets somewhere behind the station they come to a window where, with practised strokes, a man is shaving the inverted cone of a kebab spit, exposing the pink flesh beneath.

Aryan passes Ahmed's scrap of paper to him through the glass.

A gauze hat perches on the man's mahogany forehead like the prow of the ship in Genova. He squints at Aryan's paper, at the dots and scratches of the writing, at the picture of a railway line, a traffic light and a bridge; his fingers leave a watermark of grease. Through the window Aryan can see a small room with four plastic tables, each empty but for a metal cube of serviettes. The man nods them inside.

'Sit, wait here a moment,' he says, and disappears with the piece of paper out the door. The scent of meat is almost overwhelming; Kabir is over at the counter staring at the falafel balls with giant eyes.

A few moments later he returns, accompanied by a stooped old man in glasses and a white crocheted cap.

'I am Pakistani – but this man speaks Farsi,' the younger man explains.

'Are you from Iran?' the old man asks.

'Afghanistan,' Aryan says. 'But we lived in Iran for a while.'

The younger man looks at Kabir. 'Would you like to eat?' he says.

Speechless with hunger, Kabir nods.

'We have only a little money,' Aryan says.

'Don't worry,' says the man. 'You pay me one day when you come back.'

He shears layers of meat off the spit and heats the pieces on the grill, pressing them and flipping them over with the spatula, before shovelling them into an envelope of warming bread. He stuffs in onion and tomato and a fistful of shredded lettuce, drenches the lot in yoghurt, and hands one to each of the boys.

They devour them so fast that the man frowns and makes them two more. Kabir's cheeks and hands are glistening and he is grinning despite himself; Aryan cannot remember better food in his life.

The old man squints at Aryan's piece of paper. 'Your friends,' he says, 'they are not so far from here. I will show you the way.'

At a traffic light the old man points down an alley. A roadway passes overhead. 'You cross here, and turn left at the *tabacchi* on the corner,' he says. 'After that, the street is two down on your right.'

They shake the man's hand and wait for the lights. The gutter is gushing with water on the other side and they hop over it like a mountain stream.

Aryan turns to wave goodbye, but already the sunlight is glancing off the man's white cap as he disappears into the rush-hour noise.

When he turns back, Kabir has vanished.

Aryan spins around. The traffic lights are changing but the cars are already ramming through. Pedestrians are banking up on the corner, jabbering on mobile phones. A bus pulls out of the kerbside, releasing a jet of black smoke and an irritable cacophony of horns.

A movement catches Aryan's eye. It is so fast he can't tell what it is. He pushes between the pedestrians, sprints past newspaper vendors and fruit stores and dusty, boarded-up windows, till he comes to a laneway lined with garbage bins and skips. Kabir is standing between two of them, so short he is almost concealed, rifling through the contents of a handbag.

'What are you doing, Kabir?' Aryan says.

His brother looks up, abashed but also defensive.

'It was just sitting there on the top of her pram,' Kabir says. 'She didn't even notice.'

'We don't steal, Kabir! We don't do that! Are you trying to get us thrown into jail?'

'Well how are we going to get to England? How are we going to eat? I'm not going to work on any more farms.'

'We still have some money,' Aryan says. He hasn't told Kabir about the last notes in his belt. 'We are not beggars; we're not thieves.'

Kabir finds what he has been groping for amid the make-up and crayons and receipts. A blue leather wallet opens in his hand. There is a photograph of a baby on one side, and in the pockets there are euro notes, and shiny coins with gold edges and silver insides.

Aryan looks at the money: two hundred and twenty-five euros. He feels ill. Baba would have been angry and ashamed. But another part of him sees how much it would help.

'Come on,' he says. 'Drop it. Let's get out of here.'

Kabir stuffs the money in his pockets and kicks the handbag under the skip. They turn out of the lane and into the roadway, taking the direction the old man had indicated. Aryan forces back the instinct to run.

The building when they reach it is derelict.

The outside windows are broken and boarded up with

plywood. No one can have lived there for a very long time.

Aryan checks the number Ahmed had written down; the crumbling façade next door is marked 46 so this must be the right one. There is an overflowing skip in the narrow street, and behind it, a hole where an entire building once stood. It looks like the result of an explosion. Huge wooden struts bolted into triangles are all that prevent its neighbours from collapsing into the void.

Aryan sits on the step to think. A motorbike revs past, too close, splashing them with dirty water.

'We should go,' Kabir says. 'This is the wrong place.'

As they stand, a door opens in the next building. A man with the thinnest face Aryan has ever seen steps out. He starts at the sight of them and waves his arms and says something aggressive-sounding in Italian.

Aryan unfolds the paper where Ahmed has scrawled the address. He holds it out to the man.

He peers at the words beneath the grease marks, at the blue lines of the paper and Ahmed's sketched-in clues. 'Who are you?' he says, speaking in Farsi now.

Aryan swallows. 'Ahmed sent us. In Istanbul. We are Afghan. He told us to ask for Rahim.'

The man narrows his eyes. 'What do you want with Rahim?' he asks.

'Ahmed said he could help us,' Aryan says. 'We are going to England. Do you know where we can find him?'

The man pauses for a moment, assessing them. 'You'd better come inside.'

The staircase, when the man shuts the door, is so dark that Aryan has to feel his way with his feet. They clutch the banister, which is a stone ridge carved into the wall and worn as smooth as a waterfall by thousands of hands. Each step has been eroded in the middle by shoes cascading down the centuries; the wan glow of a skylight many storeys above peters out before it reaches the lower floors.

Aryan is counting. After fifty-six steps, the man unlocks a door.

A woman is inside, ironing sheets; the room smells of washing powder and steam. A baby whimpers among some cushions on the bed.

The woman sets down the iron and covers her hair and looks at the boys with wide eyes.

The man closes the door behind them. 'I am Rahim,' he says.

He asks them their names and how they met Ahmed.

'And how do you think I can help you?' he says. 'You can't stay here and we don't have any money to give you.'

Aryan feels his courage ebb. It has been a mistake to come to this place.

'Ahmed said you could tell us how to get as far as France,' he says. His voice carries no conviction.

His wife looks at Kabir, and Aryan is suddenly conscious of how ragged and dirty they are, how much like vagabonds they must appear. They have been wearing the same jeans and sweatshirts since Iran; everything they own is on their backs and full of dust. The woman says something to her husband in a language Aryan doesn't understand. The man's eyes flash; the woman keeps hers lowered. His words jab like fists; her voice is low but insistent.

'One night then,' the man says at the end of it. 'You can stay one night. But only because my wife says you look so young. After that you go. Tomorrow you go to the station. You get on the train to France. I will tell you the best way.'

'Thank you,' Aryan says.

'Don't thank me,' Rahim says. 'We already have big problems. They will get even bigger if the landlord sees you here. As soon as possible you leave.'

The apartment is just one room. There is one bed, one divan, and one window looking straight out on to a wall. The family eats, sleeps, cooks and washes in a single space. Above a cracked, yellowed sink there is a tap with hot water, and the woman uses it to fill a plastic tub so they can wash behind a curtain in the corner. She gives them each a hand towel and a T-shirt of her husband's, and when they are done she washes their clothes. The clear water quickly darkens as the Greek dirt embedded in their jeans billows in inky clouds; she has to refill the bucket several times, and empty it in the toilet down the hall, before she can rinse them clean. Both of them are wearing two sets of clothes, a tip they learned from Ahmed, so they can reverse them after the dirt of the trucks if suddenly they need to look clean.

Kabir takes one end of each pair of trousers and helps her wring them out; the four of them hang, pat-patting on to newspaper, from a line strung diagonally across the room.

'You know people in England?' Rahim asks.

'We will go to the nephew of a tailor I worked with in Iran who was born in my father's village. He is twenty and lives in London. He has a job in a restaurant with Pakistanis.'

'And what are you going to do there?'

'I want to go to school. My brother too.'

'And what do you plan to study?'

Aryan hesitates. He feels uncomfortable being the target of so many questions. There is something intrusive in the asking that makes him feel the way his father's brothers used to make him feel – powerless, pried upon, inadequate. But the family is being kind to them, and he and Kabir need their help.

'Computers,' he says softly.

The man guffaws. 'What do you know about computers?'

Aryan is confused, stung more by his tone than the words. 'We had one at school in Iran. In Istanbul I looked up the border on the Internet,' he says.

He feels his face colouring.

How can he explain that what he really loves is maths? He loves the cool, clean numbers that resolve things without the heat of emotion. He loves the way a whole equation can be pared down to a single number, as if it were hidden inside all along. He loves the way formulas can turn into geometry or graphs. But above all he loves its certainties, the way its answers exist in a quiet world impervious to anger or conflict or grief or revenge or loss.

'Well after all, why not – computers are the future, aren't they,' the man says. Aryan can't tell if his words are sarcastic or sincere. 'Even Afghanistan one day will need computers. What about him?' He nods at Kabir.

Kabir puffs up his chest. 'I'm going to be a musician,' he says. 'I will play songs for the English people at their weddings.'

The man laughs, his angular face relaxing for the first time. 'I hope they appreciate Afghan songs in England,' he says.

The woman nods towards Kabir and speaks to her husband.

'She says she will cut your hair, both of you,' Rahim says. 'She is right. They will never let you into school in England looking like goats straight down from the hills.'

Later, Rahim tells them about the trains. That they might have to get off in Nice, or Cannes, and get another train to Paris. If the police send them back to Italy they can wait and try again, or cross on foot from Ventimiglia, an Italian town on the road that runs next to the sea.

Then, in Aryan's notebook, the man draws them a map

of Paris in thick green ink that clots and smudges under his fist. He puts in a station, and a river, and a canal. He adds arrows that show where they have to walk for a couple of kilometres, until they reach a park. Beside the park he draws another station.

'This park,' Rahim says, stabbing green ballpoint dots on to the page where he has just drawn a clump of stick trees, 'is where all the Afghans meet.'

He presses so hard that the next day Aryan finds duplicate maps furrowed into the following two pages.

The intimate sound of scissor blades is close to his ear; Aryan is trying not to move. Dark crescents of hair settle on his knees like apostrophes. In his nostrils there is a tickling that wrinkling his nose won't alleviate; finally he throws up a hand, and the scissors hesitate before resuming their journey. Delicate fingertips brush his neck, tug at the hair behind his ears, check that the length is even on both sides; he is betrayed by a sudden flush of embarrassment. It is the first time anyone has touched him with such gentleness since he can remember; the feel of it mingles with the image still on his retina of the girl in the railway carriage; he wants it to last and last, and then feels ashamed at his longing. He prays the woman hasn't seen his flaming cheeks; is glad that, unlike in the barber's shop where he used to go with his father, there is no mirror here.

Kabir has already had his turn. When Aryan runs his hand upwards against the grain of his short-cropped hair, it reminds him of the puppies back on the farm. Kabir's giggles come in contagious ripples.

The tension lifts as his muscles relax in the safety and warmth of their refuge.

In the end they have to wait two days for their clothes to dry. Then Rahim directs them to the station.

In the train to France, Aryan peers at his new reflection in the lamplight, his features appearing and disappearing against the black backdrop of night.

They are still his eyes peering back at him, though the shadows around them look deeper. Perhaps his newly shortened hair is making his face look different. He knows he is changing but he can't identify exactly how. It is not only the down on his lip. He can't tell whether it is just the light, or whether his cheeks have grown thinner, his eyes larger, his jaw more gaunt.

He runs his hand along the nape of his neck, remembering the dangerous lisp of scissors, the woman's hand grazing his cheek. He remembers the girl in the night train to Rome. Their images overlap and blur, and the thought of them makes him feel happy and empty at the same time.

They awaken more than an hour from the terminal in Nice.

Their carriage rocks through tunnels and creeps through sleeping stations. They crawl past the rear of apartment blocks where women in bathrobes reach into kitchen cupboards, and shadows move behind windows thickened with steam. There are hothouses full of pumpkins and tomatoes, and carpets of cacti, and plantations of beach umbrellas where the rails pass close to the shore. Tent awnings stretch beside caravans, and rambling villas perch on headlands, among pine trees growing at perilous right-angles to the cliffs.

'Why do people have swimming pools if they live so close to the sea?' Kabir says. The aqua rectangles flash past them like postage stamps of sky.

Aryan has wedged their tickets into the net above their folded table and doesn't answer. He is thinking about the disused fountain they used to splash in after it rained, how they used to dry off by lying on the roof of an old Russian tank that heated up in the sun. How that was where he had gone to play with his friends on the day that Baba was killed.

They have followed Rahim's advice and picked out a family in the train. They plan to tag along beside them when they alight, in case there are any police.

But when the train pulls into Nice, Kabir gets blocked in the aisle by the crush of passengers, and the family disappears down the steps.

The crowd is washing them towards the exit when anxiety suddenly clutches Aryan's throat. Peaked hats and dark-blue uniforms are moving towards them; he is gripped by an involuntary fear.

'Papers,' one of the policemen says. He and Kabir are hemmed in by a sea of official blue.

Aryan produces their train tickets.

The policeman takes them, examines them, holds them up to the light. Then he rips them in half.

'Where is your passport?' he says.

'No passport,' says Aryan. His mouth is dry and he stumbles over the English words.

'Where are you from?'

'Afghanistan.'

'How old are you?'

Aryan tries to ignore the truncheon and the pistol at his waist, and the heavy boots like the ones that soldiers wear. He looks to the female officer instead. She carries the same weapons as the men, and her hair is tied back so tightly that it pulls all the expression from her face.

'Fourteen,' he says. His heart is beating fast.

The man barks something into a two-way radio. The reply comes in a screech of static.

'You know to come to France you need a passport and a visa,' the policeman says. 'You have to go home to your country and get them.'

Aryan looks at him with a kind of disbelief. In his mind their journey unspools like the ribbon of a broken cassette. He thinks about all the terrain they have covered: the months of unpaid labour in Greece, the long hours in the workshop in Turkey, the way they crossed Lake Van in a leaking boat. He thinks of the night-time struggle across the mountains, and the Kurdish peasants they stayed with, and the smugglers who left anyone who couldn't keep up by the side of the trail. He remembers the trek across the desert in Iran, his palpitating heart as they crossed the frontier by night to avoid the border patrols, and their last journey out of Afghanistan. He thinks about the things that he sold, and the money that has gone, and the things that can never be reversed.

'We don't want to stay in France,' Aryan says.

But the policeman is already pulling handcuffs out of his pocket. Aryan's stomach contracts. He looks wildly around but the police officers are standing very close. He can feel Kabir trembling at his side.

Aryan's wrists are so thin that the handcuffs have to be adjusted to the narrowest setting; the policewoman does the same for Kabir.

Blank with fear, they watch another policeman stretch his hands into skin-coloured surgical gloves. Then he pats down their bodies, searching for weapons.

Kabir is white-faced. He recoils at the man's touch. Aryan has never seen him so afraid.

They are led to the back of a police van with plastic coverings on the seats. They are driven back across the border to Italy.

'Couple more for you,' the French officer says as they enter an Italian police station. Aryan can see red-and-black playing cards aligned in columns on a computer screen.

'Where are you going then?' the Italian policeman asks

when the French van has pulled away. The buttons of his jacket strain over his paunch. Beside him, a young lieutenant scrutinizes them with the eyes of a ferret.

'England,' Aryan says.

'How old's he?' he asks, nodding towards Kabir.

'Eight,' Aryan says.

The man swears. 'They're getting younger all the time,' he says to his colleague. 'I'm not locking up kids.'

He turns to Aryan. 'Make yourself scarce,' he says. 'I don't want to see you ever again.'

Aryan guesses they are in one of the small Italian border towns they had seen from the window of the train. Maybe it is Ventimiglia, the town that Rahim mentioned. He knows Kabir will feel better if they can find something to eat.

In a narrow street they come across a shop selling takeaway pizzas and fries. Counting their coins, Aryan adds a can of Coke from the refrigerator. They sit dangling their feet on a low wall outside and ignore the seagulls clamouring for a share of their spoils.

Kabir licks the salt off his fingers and wipes his greasy hands on his trousers.

'We're going to have to walk,' Aryan says, 'like Rahim said. You feel up to it?'

'How far is it?' Kabir asks.

'The same distance we did in the van.'

Kabir ponders. 'What about your ankle?' he says.

'It's OK. We'll go slowly if it starts to hurt.'

'Maybe it'll be shorter if we go along the beach.'

They follow the cantaloupe-coloured streets to the sea. A yacht struggles to make it into shore. A trio of women gossip over prams with hoods like refugee tents. They button their cardigans to their necks as the breeze whips their skirts against their legs.

No one takes any notice of the two boys.

It is the first time they have seen the sea, apart from the glimpses they had had from the train, and the patch of blue they saw on the waterfront in Genova.

Kabir is thrilled. He gallops through sand and reefs of pebbles and calls back over his shoulder to Aryan.

'I'll race you to the water,' he says, his too-long trousers flapping against his too-short legs.

At the water's edge, where the sea-stones clatter and slide, he tangles in his own momentum and trips. He comes up frowning, rubbing the imprint of pebbles off dented knees.

Aryan laughs. 'Nice dive!' he calls.

'I won!' Kabir says when he catches his breath, raising his fist in triumph at Aryan's approach. 'Do you think it's really salt?'

'Check and let me know.'

Kabir spits out the briny water with a grimace.

'You may as well go all the way in now,' Aryan says, observing the high-water mark on Kabir's jeans.

'Brrrrr – too cold!' he says. 'Why is the sea two-colours blue?'

'I don't know,' Aryan says. 'Maybe the dark part is where the sharks are waiting for you to come in.'

'Or you, if I push you in first!'

They tussle on the sand where the pebbles end, Kabir twisting Aryan's fingers to win the advantage. But Aryan easily slides a knee on to his chest.

'Mercy, do you beg for mercy?' Aryan asks. 'Or shall I feed you to the sharks?'

'Never!' says Kabir, squirming.

Aryan leans more weight on to his knee. 'Will you eat sand?' His hand forms a funnel above Kabir's face.

Kabir wriggles his head from side to side. 'Peace!' Kabir says. 'Peace! You win.'

'Promise to be my slave?' The hand hovers.

'Yes, anything!' Kabir says.

'Say it!'

'I promise to be your slave!'

'For ever?'

'Yes, yes, I promise to be your slave for ever!' Kabir cries. Aryan relinquishes his grip.

Coming up breathless, Kabir pulls the cone of a seashell from under his back.

'Just tricking,' he says. 'I'll never be your slave!'

Aryan fells him again and tickles him till they are distracted by the valiant yacht, which finally manages to ground itself in the shallows.

It is late afternoon when they start walking. Occasionally they see a train flash between the houses or vanish into a tunnel with a flick of its silver tail.

The breeze picks up and caps the blue sea white.

It is heavy going through the sand. Their shoes fill up and every step takes more effort than they had thought. After a while the beach turns completely into pebbles but their feet wobble on the rickety stones and Aryan is worried he will twist his ankle again.

When they come to a stream feeding effluent into the sea they leave the beach and walk along the quiet roads between the holiday homes. The summer has faded, and many of the cottages are already boarded up.

As evening draws in they take some late tomatoes from an unwatched market garden and make a nest out of newspapers and dried grass.

Aryan is dreaming. It is night and he is on his own, outside a strange villa, high above the sea.

He has slipped over the wall, over the tripwire, and crunched across stones unfazed by the sudden flash of floodlights, a trespasser on a continent not his own. The howling of neighbouring dogs jars in the scented night air but they are too far off to trouble him now. Dappled in the artificial light, he stands in the shadow of a magnolia; bathed in its perfume, he drapes his clothes over the shrubbery like an offering. His naked skin puckers in the cool evening air; the tiles are smooth under his ruined feet. For a moment he pauses on the edge, just for a heartbeat, just for a breath. Then, in one luxurious movement, he arches and dives, shredding the silver blueness and the anxiety that never leaves him now into splinters of shuddering light.

The shock of the water winds him. He has never learnt to swim yet he is swimming; only if he keeps moving will his muscles fool him into forgetting the cold. Slipstreams of bubbles slake off his hands in whirling mercury pods; the dirt that seems to fill every pore dissolves with his exhaustion, so that all that aches inside him is momentarily soothed. He feels his tiredness lifting like the ghost of the dead. The pool is lit from the sides, behind bulbous fish-eye glass; where the tiled floor drops away it seems like he is swimming upward through space, powering towards the light of distant suns.

He wakes early and sits up, his back to the gnarled bark of a tree, watching the ants, waiting for Kabir to open his eyes. His brother's plump cheeks are damp with the moisture of his breathing. The dawn is tangy with iodine and the smell of tomato leaves.

A caterpillar pleats and stretches itself along the length of a branch like a tape measure with audacious stripes.

Not the dream but the feeling of the dream floats back to him as the day unfolds; he was the swimmer but it also wasn't him – like a strange voice from the future, it seems to Aryan to be an intimation of the person he is yet to become.

The feeling of it accompanies him all day, this presence of his future self. It walks with him as they follow the road into France, skirting the craggy mountains whose outcrops tumble into the sea.

Guard dogs rear on their hind legs in a paroxysm of barking as they pass.

They reach the outskirts of Nice in the middle of the afternoon.

They follow a tramline past orange apartment blocks and manicured parks where palm trees and pines compete. Aryan can't work out what the climate here must be, with desert plants and mountain trees growing side by side as if the land itself were uncertain whether it was a place of heat or ice.

Suddenly, through a gap in the apartment buildings, the sky begins to open out; beyond them, he senses, must be the sea.

A chill breeze tugs at their clothes and whips the hotel flags. White sun loungers bask in empty rows on the pebbles, waiting for better days. Aryan is amazed that no one has stolen them; not one of them is locked up.

Aryan hasn't got a plan. He just wants to be invisible while they work out how to get to the station, and how to buy a ticket to Paris without encountering the police.

'Let's walk along a bit,' he says.

The sea wall rises high above them, and above that, the

waterfront hotels of Nice. A woman jogs by on the promenade; Aryan is embarrassed at the sight of her lycra-clad body. An old man throws a stick to a dog that retrieves it despite the fringe over its eyes.

'I wish Tom and Jerry were here,' Kabir says. It's the first time he has mentioned the puppies since they escaped from the farm in Greece.

'They'd have gone crazy with all the seaweed,' Aryan says. 'Dogs like smelly stuff like that.'

'Maybe we can have a dog when we get to England,' Kabir says. 'They love dogs over there. Even the Queen has dogs.'

'The Queen! What do you know about the Queen?' Aryan asks.

'She takes them hunting. Hamid told me. She even lets her dogs inside her castle.'

'And how would Hamid know that?'

'He showed me a photograph in a Turkish magazine. She was sitting on a blue sofa and the dogs were on the sofa next to her.'

'Hamid and his stories,' Aryan says. He is amazed at the things Kabir remembers, and wonders when it was that he and Hamid had found time to discuss the Queen of England's pets.

'It's true!' Kabir says. 'Why would he make up something like that?'

'I didn't say he made it up,' Aryan says. 'I'd just like to see that picture too.'

They sit on the pebbles on the waterfront lobbing smooth grey missiles into the waves.

'Maybe we could go to England by speedboat,' Kabir says.

'Oh yes, and where are we going to get a speedboat?' says Aryan.

'There's one right there.'

Aryan laughs and jabs him in the ribs. 'Can someone as crazy as you really be my brother?'

'Why not? I think it's a good plan.'

'Do you have any idea how far it is? We'd have to go right across the Mediterranean, and all around the outside of Europe,' he says. 'It's miles and miles and miles.'

'I guess we'd need a lot of petrol,' Kabir says.

'Not to mention navigation equipment. And supplies. And a boat so strong it could withstand the Atlantic storms. We'd end up like the *Titanic*.'

'It wouldn't be like the *Titanic* because it's too warm for icebergs.'

'Icebergs would be the least of our worries,' Aryan says. 'But hey, let me know when you get any other bright ideas.'

'OK, so you think of something better.' Kabir's shoulders slump and he turns his back the way he always does when he feels sulky or hurt.

Hunger is making them irritable. Aryan is beginning to wonder where they will spend the night.

'Come on,' Aryan says, wobbling to his feet on the clackety stones.

They climb the steps in the sea wall and follow a narrow street behind the promenade in search of a bakery.

'How many euros have we got left?' Kabir says. Most of the money Kabir stole in Rome went to pay for their train tickets to France.

'We've still got a few,' Aryan says. The large silver coins nestle flat and warm in his hand. He has €46.50 distributed among his pockets and shoes, and €340 in his belt, and if what Rahim said was right, they will need all of it and more when they get to Calais.

Noses pressed to a window, their eyes stretch in wonder. There are fantastical constructions that look too beautiful to eat – glazed strawberries pinned to rafts of meringue with the tiniest seam of orange; circular cakes iced with chocolate as shiny as mirrors and smudged with fragments of gold; small battalions of raspberries marshalled on biscuit plains.

'Are people here so rich they eat gold?'

'Maybe it just looks like gold,' Aryan says. 'Or maybe they've invented some sort of edible gold paint.'

Before they have time to consider it, Aryan is spinning on his heels.

A man in a suntan and slip-on shoes is walking past, arguing in Farsi with a woman in a bright floral skirt.

'The view of the sea was fantastic, just like in that Matisse painting,' the man is saying in an accent Aryan recognizes from Tehran. 'But the bathroom was terrible, like all these bathrooms in Europe.'

'There was nothing wrong with that shower,' the woman says. 'You were just too impatient with the settings.'

Aryan grabs Kabir by the arm and hurries after them.

'Sir, sir,' Aryan says to the man's retreating back.

The man doesn't hear and walks on.

'Sir,' Aryan says again. He darts to one side, dares to tug the man's sleeve.

The man halts in surprise. The woman takes a step backwards.

'Excuse me, sir, are you from Iran?' Aryan says.

'No, we're American. Though you are right, we are originally from Iran. What can we do for you?'

'Please,' Aryan says. 'Can you help us?'

The man looks at the woman beside him. 'Are you boys in some kind of trouble?'

'We are hungry,' says Aryan.

The man and the woman exchange glances.

'This is my wife,' the man says. 'Where are you from?'

'Afghanistan,' says Aryan.

'And what are two boys from Afghanistan doing here in Nice?'

'We are going to England,' Aryan says.

'So we can go to school,' adds Kabir.

'Is this your brother?' the woman asks.

Aryan touches his heart with his right hand and extends it to the man and to the woman, and tells them their names.

'How old are you?' the woman says.

'I'm fourteen and my brother is eight,' says Aryan.

'And where are your parents?' the woman asks.

The question comes as a jolt. No one has asked him this before.

'They both died,' Aryan says. 'In the war.'

The man and woman speak to each other in English. The woman smiles at Kabir and tousles his short-cropped hair.

Only Aryan noticed Kabir flinch when the man went to shake his hand.

They are seated inside a noisy bistro in a square ringed with restaurants overlooking a fountain. Outside, the breeze nags at the corners of tablecloths pegged down with metal clips, and teases the coloured napkins folded into empty glasses. Heaters on tall poles beam wastefully down at the tables, but the breeze defeats the feeble sunshine. All the metal chairs are empty; even the seagulls look forlorn.

The woman is running a finger down the menu; Kabir stares at her cyclamen-pink nails. 'What do you boys feel like eating?' she says. 'They have everything here: schnitzel, fettuccine, steaks ...'

Aryan swallows. The Americans-from-Iran are kind but he doesn't know any of these things. Kabir is swinging his feet from the chair.

Her husband sees Aryan's confusion. 'Why don't you order for the two of them?' he says.

The woman brightens. 'All right,' she says. 'I think minestrone, and then beefburgers for the boys. And maybe apple juice. How does that sound?'

Aryan is anxious this French food will have pork inside it.

'It's OK here,' the lady says. 'We don't eat it either.'

Kabir's cheeks are red with the warmth of the bistro and glisten with burger juice.

Aryan can't remember the last time he ate like this, hot food in a warm place, his belly taut with contentment. Happiness creeps over him like the dawn.

He tells the Americans they used to live in Iran and that's where he went to school, though Kabir was too small to go.

The lady's eyes look suddenly sad. Aryan wonders if he has said something wrong.

The man says they live in Los Angeles now and have been on a Mediterranean cruise. They flew from America to Nice and caught the train to Marseilles, and boarded a big ship that took them to Barcelona. From there they sailed to Tunis, Malta, Alexandria, Athens, Naples, Rome and Genoa. Funny, the man says, how these towns in Europe have more than one name – in Italy they call Genoa 'Genova', and in France they call it 'Genes'.

'We were in Genova,' Kabir says, eyes shining. 'The buildings are like jails and there are black men selling handbags and it's the first time we saw the sea.'

The woman smiles. 'We saw the handbag-sellers too,' she says. Her voice moves up and down and sounds to Aryan like a sort of song. 'They were in the port. I bought a wooden frog for my daughter.' And she produces the small carving from her handbag.

Kabir's face lights up. 'Maybe it came from Solomon,' he says.

'Solomon?' The woman raises her eyebrows.

'He was one of the handbag-sellers we met,' Aryan says. 'He was meant to buy us tickets for the train.'

On the ship the Americans had a cabin with a porthole and from their bunks they could see the lights of the coast-line slipping past them during the night. Every day they woke up in a different country. Finally they disembarked in Genoa and caught the train to Nice.

Now, the lady says, they are going to spend some days in Paris before flying home.

Aryan can't imagine going to so many places just for fun.

The woman says they have children in America, a daughter just a bit older than Aryan, and a son of seventeen. She shows them a photograph in her wallet. Aryan sees a girl with oval eyes and long straight hair, and a boy in a blue-and-white cap.

'He's in his sports gear,' the man says. 'He is crazy about that game.'

The woman laughs and says the picture is out of date. 'They're both a bit bigger now,' she says.

There were no photographs in Aryan's family, except for the one in his wallet. He thinks about showing it to the Americans, but there would be too many things to explain.

'They are staying with their cousins in Los Angeles,' the man continues. 'One day you should come to America to meet them.'

'Can you go there in a ship with portholes?' Kabir asks.

The woman smiles. 'It's best to fly,' she says. 'Otherwise it would take too long.'

Aryan can't believe it would take longer than the time it has taken him and Kabir to get from Afghanistan to France. He can't imagine what it would be like to go to America in a plane.

After the meal, the man asks when they are travelling to Paris.

'In the next few days, ins'allah,' Aryan says. He is wondering how they will be able to get a ticket if the police are patrolling the station again.

'Why don't you come with us?' the man says. 'We have a train tomorrow afternoon at two.'

Aryan hesitates. 'We don't have much money for tickets,' he says. He is worried about their dwindling funds.

The man waves a dismissive hand. 'I think we can handle that,' he says.

Aryan looks at Kabir's shining face. They must be the luckiest boys in the world.

'We would be very happy to go with you,' he says.

The woman says something elliptical to her husband in English.

'Yes,' he says to her, and turns to the boys. 'First we must get you some new clothes.'

Aryan doesn't realize how much he has grown until he sees himself in the full-length mirror in the cubicle. He is thinner but taller now. The threadbare jeans that the woman washed for him in Rome hang off his haunches, even despite the second pair he is wearing underneath.

Aryan's feet have grown too. His toes have bored holes through the tips of his trainers.

But above all it's his face that startles him now that he can see it in the light. It's thinner, and there are the lines of an old man around his eyes.

'For a fourteen-year-old he's a bit small,' the shop assistant is telling the woman in fragmented English, blue jeans draped over her right arm, black jeans over the left.

The American woman ignores her.

'Which colour?' she asks Aryan, taking the jeans from the assistant and poking them through the curtain; her cyclamen nails are luminous against the cloth. He is frightened that one of the two will suddenly whip the curtain open and expose him, half naked, in his ragged underwear.

He pulls the black pair through the gap and unlaces his trainers. He is suddenly embarrassed by the odour released by shoes he has worn constantly for months. The tread on the bottom is worn as smooth as river-stone. He moves quickly, sliding both jeans off together, dragging on the stiff new trousers, flushed.

'Come out and show me,' the woman says, too polite to comment on the smell. Socks, undershorts, a football shirt and a top with a hood form a soft pyramid in her arms. 'Turn around,' she says.

The fit, she decides, is good. 'Here, put all of these on, if you like them,' she says. Aryan is grateful for her briskness.

He inhales the chemical scent of newness. Aryan has never had clothes from a shop. In Afghanistan their mother made their shirts and trousers, once a year in springtime, from a single bolt of fabric for all her sons. When they moved to Iran, he and Kabir had had to discard their Afghan clothes for Western ones, to blend in better in a place fed up with so many arrivals from Iraq and Afghanistan. The garments their cousins gave them had been washed and worn many times.

These French clothes have fold lines down the front, and cardboard tickets that scratch his neck, and heavy white plastic triangles that pull them out of shape. Aryan is not sure about the jeans. They are stiff enough to stand up by themselves.

'They'll get softer as you wear them,' the American woman says, as if reading his thoughts.

Kabir has not yet lost all of his puppy fat. The shop assistant is kneeling to fold up the cuffs of his jeans. He is beaming in a red-and-blue T-shirt with Spiderman on the front; over the top he has a dark-blue hooded sweatshirt with the number 42 in yellow on the back.

The American lady asks the shop assistant to snip off the labels so they can wear their new clothes right away. She takes the cardboard tickets to the till.

'Have you checked the pockets?' she asks them. She raises an eyebrow but makes no remark at the double sets of clothes they are stuffing into the carrier bags.

Aryan goes through his and Kabir's old trousers one more time. He transfers their last euro coins to his new pockets; his belt with its diminished wad of notes he eases through the loops of his new jeans; from Kabir's pockets he salvages a seashell, and the blue plastic warrior from the train.

Opposite, in a sports store, they buy new shoes. Aryan's trainers are black. The soles have so much bounce he feels like a moonwalker defying gravity with every step. Kabir chooses a luminous red with jagged white stripes down the sides.

'Ready?' the American woman says.

She drops their old gear into a rubbish bin in the street.

'Aryan, when's my birthday?'

'Your what?'

'My birthday. You told the Americans I was eight. But if they ask me which day, how will I remember when I was born?'

'I've already told you that,' Aryan says.

'Yes but I want you to tell me again.'

Aryan sighs. 'You remember,' he says. 'First there is the snow. Then the snow melts, and it gets a little bit warm. And then after that is when you were born.'

Kabir ponders this. 'So how do you know I am eight?'

'Because I've been counting,' Aryan says. 'Plus I'm older than you, remember. There have been eight winters since you were born. And in case you don't believe me, Baba was counting too.'

'Am I the same age here as in Afghanistan?'

'Of course you are. It doesn't matter that they've got another calendar here. In Europe they just start counting on a different day. But the same number of years have still gone by.'

'Aryan?'

'Yes, Kabir.'

'Do they have snow in England?'

'I don't know, Kabir.'

'But what if they don't have snow in England? How will I know how old I am?'

'They have months in England. January, February, April, like that,' Aryan says. 'When we get there we will choose one that's after the winter. That way you can keep track.'

Illuminated by the floodlights, a flock of seagulls bobs in the black water like blown-off paper hats, all of them turned identically into the wind. People sit in small clusters on the beach, watching a pair of fishermen cast oversized rods into the sea.

The grey pebbles chatter under their feet. Aryan wonders how far down they'd have to dig to reach the sand.

Kabir stumbles as they make their way back to the place where, earlier, the sun loungers were lying on the stones. Someone has strung them loosely together on a long thin chain. Aryan leans two of them on their sides, face to face, and wedges them into the pebbles to make a windbreak near the beach-café wall. He places a third one beside them, pushing it low into the stones, and covers it with a flattened cardboard box that somebody left in the street.

Aryan's back is cold but at least his front is protected. As they lie down to sleep, he hugs his brother for warmth. His hair smells of salt and wind and Kabir.

'I like hearing the waves,' Kabir says, long after Aryan has explained to him about his birthday, long after Aryan thinks he has gone to sleep. 'It's like the sea is breathing.'

All night, the wind makes a hissing noise in Aryan's ear as it tries to whip the cardboard away. The cold keeps him awake for a long time. Perhaps he should have told the Americans, when they asked, that he and Kabir did need somewhere to sleep. But the couple had already given them so much, and Aryan didn't want to feel any further obliged.

He buries his face in his sweatshirt, breathing in the unfamiliar smell. The clothes make him feel different, the same person but prouder of himself, like someone who doesn't have to hide.

He tries to imagine what it would be like to sleep in a cabin on board a ship, to watch the lights of mysterious cities glide by through a porthole, and wake up every morning in the same bed but in a new place.

Because they are not sure of the time, Aryan and Kabir go early to the park opposite the Americans' hotel and wait on the benches under the pine trees and the green and orange palms.

Aryan makes Kabir practise the English words he has taught him to pass the time.

'Eag-le,' Kabir repeats. 'Shep-herd. Snow.'

Then they rehearse English counting.

'I can't keep any more words in my head,' Kabir says after they get to twenty.

'But you remember where we're going, Soldierboy?' Aryan says.

'KabulTehranIstanbulAthensRomeParisLondon.' Kabir says it all in one breath. 'You see, Aryan,' he says. 'I won't forget.'

Aryan only trusted the capital cities, the names he had memorized himself before teaching Kabir. There were other places they had heard of, and places they had passed through in between, like Van, and Genova, and now Nice. But the big cities were where the connections were, where they could always find other Afghans, where there were bus stations and people smugglers and trains.

It is strange, Aryan thinks, how each place they cross

leaves impressions that are different from the pictures he had in his head before they arrive. Tehran was filled with skyscrapers and snow-covered mountains, but what he remembers most is the refuse piled up in the canal, and the thrum of engines belching exhaust at the bus station. Istanbul, where he had imagined men in fezzes and curly-toed slippers, is the whirr of sewing machines, and a mosque of gleaming gold. In Iran he had seen a picture of the Acropolis, but in Athens he only glimpsed the real thing once, rearing above the pollution, at the far end of a street that ran away from Alexandras Park. Instead, what he remembers of Athens is the moving stairs in the metro, and the plumbing in their cheap hotel. Of Rome – city of gladiators and lions – he remembers the one-room apartment of Ahmed's friend and his wife who cut their hair.

They stockpile seeds from the flowerbeds and fire them at a beer can with a slingshot they fashion from elastic bands discarded by the postman. They watch the street cleaners go by in long-hosed vehicles that send Kabir into a fit of giggling because they look like small green elephants with oversized trunks.

When the Americans come out, Aryan jumps up. He sees them looking up and down the street until they spot them in the park and beckon to them to cross.

A man with gold braid on his sleeves is loading the Americans' luggage into the back of a taxi. He holds the door open as they clamber inside.

At the station they wait with the American woman while her husband goes to the ticket window. Then they stand all together on the platform.

Two policemen in dark glasses lean on the bars around the exit, watching passengers get on and off the trains. There is a dog on a leash at their side.

Aryan's mouth goes dry and his stomach tenses. Their truncheons hang like unspoken threats from their belts; the butts of their black revolvers sit sinister as reptiles at their hips.

'Don't look at them,' Aryan tells Kabir. He is relieved they are not the same officers who sent them back before.

Following its silver snout along the rails, the fast train to Paris slides in. With the Americans, they scramble up the steps.

The train winds along the coast for ages before heading north. They pass wide rivers, and churches on distant outcrops, and endless open plains. Aryan thinks France must be the flattest country he has ever seen.

Disappearing through the carriages, the woman returns with cheese sandwiches and tins of orange drink.

They say goodbye to the Americans on the steps of the Gare de Lyon station in Paris.

'We'll be staying on the Champs-Elysées for three days,' the man says. 'That's where we'll be if you come by.'

Aryan touches his heart and shakes their hands and thanks them. They have to find the other Afghans and work out how to get to England, he says. Then they will come and say hello.

'Are you sure you have a place to go now?' the woman asks.

Aryan nods. He has Rahim's green-pen map in his notebook.

The couple wave to them from the side window of their taxi as it sweeps in a wide arc down the concourse.

A man at a bus stop points them towards the river. They walk between it and a flyover until they find the place where the canal empties into the Seine. They take a metal staircase down to a walkway along the water's edge, where pleasure craft and longboats lie anchored along the sides of the canal.

People are sitting on the decks laughing and drinking. It takes Aryan a moment to work out why it all looks back to front: the plants are growing on the inside, the tables and chairs are on the outside, and the bicycles are parked up on the roofs.

Up ahead, there are trains going past above the water but under the road; out of sight, a chorus of police sirens wails.

When the water disappears they climb another staircase to an enormous traffic circle with a golden angel on top of a pillar. People in long scarves sit smoking on café terraces; a curved building made of metal and glass reflects the autumn sky.

Aryan takes out Rahim's sketch and shows Kabir. The canal must run under the wide road up ahead, where the traffic flows on either side of the flowerbeds and a double row of trees. Curled leaves lie upturned on the pavement like half-open hands.

Several times they stop. Kabir's new shoes are giving him blisters and Aryan is walking too fast. He ties Kabir's laces tighter to stop the rubbing but still he drags his feet. Aryan piggybacks him till he gets too tired. They stop to watch a group of men playing a game with metal balls. Further on, fountains of water shoot skywards like a pod of underground whales.

Steering wide of the wild-eyed men shouting abuse at invisible demons, they find an empty bench where Kabir can undo his laces. He shakes a pebble out of his shoe.

Through the trees up ahead they see an intersection. Beyond it, the water of the canal reappears.

Aryan's spirits lift. 'It can't be too far now,' he says.

A steep green bridge arches over the water. They climb to the top and lean over the rails. On the edges of the water below, people are smoking and playing guitars. There are restaurant tables on the footpaths, and rollerbladers slaloming between the pedestrians and the waiters. People speed by on bicycles, tinkling their bells.

'Look at that!' Kabir says.

A boat half full of tourists appears in the water below them, waiting to pass through the lock. Passers-by gape as a boom falls like the border between two countries, halting the stream of motorbikes and cars. They stand, transfixed, as water rushes in and the heads of the tourists rise to the level of the banks. Suddenly the bridge splits apart and turns on a pivot, and the boatload of tourists floats past under their feet.

Two children about Kabir's age lean far out over the edge, trying to scoop up the water with their hands. Their mothers, when they notice, shriek and haul them back in.

'Do you think that boat goes to England?' Kabir asks.

Aryan laughs. 'Yeah, sure, twice a week from Kabul,' he says.

They watch as it disappears into the next lock, and vanishes under the road along which they've just walked.

Aryan starts down the steps of the bridge.

'Come on,' he says, turning back. 'See that fence? I think we've reached the park.'

Three youths are perched on the low stone wall of the canal. Aryan can tell they are Afghans, even from a distance, even before hearing them speak.

'Do you know if there is anywhere we can sleep?' he says. 'We've only just arrived.'

The three look up. 'For underage boys like you, there is a place, but it's too late for today,' says one of them. He disentangles a mobile phone from his pocket and looks at the time inscribed over the photo of a Bollywood actress.

'You have to be there before eight o'clock to get in,' says his friend. He has a round face and wide-spaced eyes and a jacket with an enormous number of zips. 'Otherwise you will have to bed down like us, out here in the park.'

Another night under the stars, Aryan thinks. Luckily they slept a bit in the train.

'Is there any place we can get something to eat?' he says.

The youths shrug. Looking at them, Aryan thinks they could be eighteen or nineteen, but the lines on their faces make them seem older. One of them is swimming inside an anorak several sizes too big.

'There is a soup kitchen further up the canal but you have to go there at half past six. There'll be nobody there now,' the man with the zippers says.

The temperature is starting to drop. People sitting along the canal wrap themselves in their jackets and scarves; old ladies, miniature dogs squeezed into the crooks of their arms, punch numbers into the walls of nearby buildings; the heavy doors click open, then slam shut.

'If you can wait till lunchtime they bring meals for homeless people to the gates of the park,' says the man with the phone, waving the Bollywood actress towards a bandstand and a cluster of trees. 'Or there's a supermarket around the corner that throws out lots of food.'

The youth with the zips holds out his hand. 'Here, you can have my bread,' he says.

Aryan thanks him and opens the white plastic bag. Inside are three disks of bread so light they feel weightless in his palm.

Aryan and Kabir demolish the bread where they stand.

A few crumbs float like snowflakes on to the flagstones beneath their feet.

As night falls, the youths show them where to climb over the park's high railings, though Aryan is so thin he can fit between the bars. They drop softly on to the mulchy soil. The man in the anorak stumbles, crushing a clump of irises underfoot.

People sitting under heaters at the outdoor restaurants barely notice the shadows slipping over the rails, or bedding down on the strange rubbery surface beneath the playground swings.

The three slide flattened cardboard boxes from behind the creepers that spill over the park's stone wall. Silently they extract plastic sacks, swollen into enormous pumpkins with bundles of bedding, from their hiding place in a tangle of shrubs.

Aryan and Kabir have nothing to lie on and nothing to pull over themselves. But there are other sheets of cardboard concealed against the wall by other men. Aryan hesitates a moment, then slides one out and hands it to Kabir. He takes a second one for himself, and they drag them away from where their owners might come looking for them. They position them close to the place the youths have chosen, in a curve of shrubbery that shields them from the wind. Aryan buttons Kabir's anorak to his chin and pulls his hood over his head and the two of them curl up, waiting for sleep.

'Tomorrow it will be better,' Aryan says. 'We will find the underage sleeping place.'

'What is underage?' Kabir asks.

'It means under eighteen.'

'What happens when you turn eighteen?' Kabir asks.

'That's when they say you are a man.'

'And then you can sleep in the park?'

Aryan laughs. 'Everything's back to front in Paris,' he says. 'They keep their animals inside their houses, the bridges break in half when a boat comes by, and the boats have to go under the roads.'

Kabir ponders the contradictions. 'What about the lights?' he says after a while.

'What lights?' Aryan says.

'The lights of the city. Ahmed said Paris was a city full of lights.'

Aryan looks around them; all he can see are the dark trees, and the streetlamps winking through the branches. 'Maybe you have to go downtown,' he says.

Paris, he remembers it now, is the bride of all the cities – that's another thing Ahmed had said. He had imagined a girl in a long white dress with a voluminous train studded with diamonds and crystals.

He stares up at the sky, wondering whether Ahmed is still in Istanbul, or somewhere ahead of them or behind them on the road.

'Those stars. It's the charioteer – the one we saw in Iran – do you remember?' he says.

Kabir follows the line of Aryan's gaze. Above the trees, the night sky has been erased by the aura of the city. But finally he makes out part of the constellation, beyond the haze of urban light.

'They're our stars,' Kabir says. 'A charioteer for travellers like us.'

'Yes just like us – except we don't have a chariot,' Aryan says.

Kabir ignores him. 'Maybe Masood and Zohra are looking at them right now, over there in Iran,' he says.

Aryan listens with half an ear. He is thinking about the night sky in Afghanistan, how he used to count the shooting stars when, long ago, he slept up on the roof on the hottest nights of the year.

'Maybe they are even thinking of us,' Kabir is saying. 'Maybe if we think hard enough we can send them a message.'

'What would you say in your message?'

'I'd tell them about the puppies and that we got new clothes and that soon we'll be going to school in England.'

There are more than a hundred men lining up for food that comes in a white truck with a big red shield on the doors. It parks between the canal and an overhead railway line, and is filled with shelves of trays that men and women distribute from trestle tables set up behind barricades.

There are not only Afghans in the queue, but Iraqis and Iranians and Kurds, and some French people who don't have a home. The youths at the back push, and the men -from the van shout, and finally they get warm pasta and hot tea.

An Afghan teenager who was behind them in the line takes Aryan and Kabir to the meeting place for the underage camp. There are Hazaras and Pashtuns and Tajiks, and a couple of boys from Africa, and they all give their names to a lady with glasses who puts them down on a list.

It is the first time since school in Iran that Aryan has seen so many boys his own age. He looks at them with a mixture of shyness and fascination. One is slumped miserably inside a phone box; some are clowning and relaxed; some are trying to pretend they're invisible inside their hoods.

The French lady and a man put Aryan and Kabir with the smallest boys and the ones who are the most tired because they have just arrived. Some of the boys laugh and jostle and try to slip their friends into the queue; the French people when they realize have to start counting all over again.

'What happens to them?' Aryan asks, nodding to a dozen others who are turned away once twenty-five of them are marshalled against a wall.

The teenager beside him shrugs. 'They have to find their own place,' he says. 'In the park, or under the bridges, or along the canal.'

They follow the two adults in an elastic line that elongates as they walk – along the canal, across a bridge and down streets so narrow they can't all fit on the pavement. Some of them stop for cyclists and miss the traffic lights. They bunch up again at a metro station enclosed by a metal grille. When a watchman winches it open, they descend a steep flight of stairs, and heap their sneakers together at the bottom in a pungent pile.

'Don't worry, they don't use it as a station any more,' the teenager says. A shock of hair flops over eyes so round they look permanently surprised; he says his name is Jawad. 'It's for homeless people in the day, and in the night it's for us.'

Inside the metro station there are no windows. But the lights are bright, and imaginary forests and islands have been painted on the walls.

Those who haven't eaten are given pasta and yoghurt on a plastic tray.

'You have to be quick for the showers,' says Jawad, showing them the way.

A young man distributes soap and toothbrushes and combs, and razors for those who need them, and an assortment of multicoloured towels.

There is a background hum of washing machines as boys in T-shirts and sweatpants wait for their clothes to come back clean and dry. The odour of disinfectant wafts under the door as the lady with the glasses swabs grazes and cuts and wounds. From a medical chest she extracts two plasters for the blisters on Kabir's heels.

Kabir's face is glowing and his hair is damp from the steam.

Jawad takes them to the cupboard for the foam mattresses they unfold on the floor, and the sleeping bags they unroll for the night.

Lying on his side in the darkness, Aryan listens to the trains prowling the tunnels on the other side of the wall. At first their eerie rumbling unnerves him; they remind him of army tanks, of restless underworld beasts. But he reminds himself that here they are safe, that his belly has stopped growling, that they are warm, and dry, and clean.

Amid the snufflings and snorings around him, he falls almost immediately into a dreamless sleep that is punctuated only occasionally by the cries of some other boy.

Shortly before midnight it starts to rain.

The first droplets sprinkle the grey footpath with black confetti. Soon there is no greyness left at all; the drops meet, overlap, then cover the surface entirely, then seek out new depressions to explore. At the top of the stairs a cavity begins to fill; the water collects patiently, inevitably; it is not ready, it is gathering volume, it is mustering strength. The surface of the pool shivers as it grows. Behind it, smaller reservoirs catch, and swell, and overflow into rivulets that burrow under leaves and cigarette butts and the wings of moths that they shoulder like trophies wrested from a battalion of ants. Searching, searching, the rivulets merge and feed into a dam that deepens behind the lip of the top stair. Its convex body trembles, hesitates, holds a moment, then tips into a cascade of storm-water that pours down step after step and across the landing and down again until it pools in lakes under the worn-out shoes of twenty-five sleeping boys.

'Why are there so many homeless people in Paris?' Kabir asks.

Aryan, too, is surprised to see so many men sleeping on top of the warm air vents in the street.

'Maybe they lost their families,' he says.

During the day the park fills up with people. Children climb and tangle and push and shout and slide on the play-ground equipment. Parents dart to break their fall. Friends turn their faces to the autumn sun and saddle the green hillocks with rugs.

On the highest knolls little girls stretch out and roll downhill in the luminous grass. At the bottom they lie giggling till the Earth stops spinning and point upwards at the giddy clouds.

There is a scrabbling and a heaving and the sound of sneakers skidding on a gravelly court. Jawad and Aryan and Kabir are watching the older Afghans play five-a-side football against a gang of Paris teenagers who have taught them the rules; their noses and the pads of their fingers poke through the quadrilateral wire.

Aryan follows the attacks and counter-attacks with a

kind of ache. His feet itch for the thrill and thrust of it. But the men are bigger than he is, and the game is too rough and fast.

One of the players limps off the court and heads to the drinking fountain. Glassy comets fly in all directions as he shakes his water-soaked hair.

Later, when the sun drops behind the buildings and the families have retreated and the last footballers are flagging and winding up their game, it takes Aryan a moment to locate Kabir.

Then he sees him, a lone figure clad in a red and blue T-shirt, rolling over and over till the contours of the land catch him and the soft earth slows him and brings him to a halt on the swirling, phosphorescent grass.

Two weeks afterwards they get off the train from Paris in the glowering dusk.

There is an icy wind that has sent the police who patrol the station exits off duty early for the day. Already the streetlights are on as they step, directionless and disoriented, into the town and walk briskly against the flow of traffic. Movement, Aryan hopes, will make them invisible as he tries to work out where to go. The shops are closing and their workers are hurrying home; cars hurl muddied water on to the footpaths as they pass.

Aryan tenses as a police car cruises by and involuntarily tightens his grip on Kabir's wrist; his brother winces and wriggles his hand free. The vehicle glides past without stopping, shattering bright, reflective puddles in the oily streets.

The Afghans they talked to in Paris said Calais was full of migrants, and that any one of them would show them where to go. But in this freezing city at nightfall, no one who looks like a migrant is anywhere in sight.

'Where's everybody gone?' Kabir says.

'Let's just keep walking,' says Aryan.

They come to a park where small clumps of snow, pockmarked by rain, have retreated under the trees. Crossing it, they follow a row of red-brick houses with remnants of snow on their roofs. It leads them back behind the railway line. The road doglegs left; straight ahead, a metal gate closes off a building site. Aryan gives Kabir a leg-up and clambers after him. Ahead looms a row of old warehouses; a sign hangs lopsidedly from a screw under one of the eaves.

As they approach the building they hear shouts and a scuffling of feet. Suddenly a ball comes flying towards them from between two walls, glancing drunkenly off the water-filled potholes. Instinctively Aryan stops it with his left foot just as the thinnest African youth he has ever seen flies out in chase. At the sight of the boys he skids to a stop. He wears a diamond in his ear and a bright red football shirt that says 'Umbro'.

With a quick movement Aryan passes him the ball that is made of faded lime-green plastic and could have done with a little air.

'Who are you?' the African asks, eyes wary, clamping the ball with his foot.

'We just got here,' Aryan says. 'We're looking for a place to spend the night.'

'Where are you from then?'

'Afghanistan.'

A shout comes from behind the wall. A player runs out and the youth shoots the dented ball towards him.

'Well you're in the wrong place. This isn't the Jungle, you know.'

Aryan is at a loss. He can see there aren't any trees.

'The Afghan camp is in the Jungle,' the boy says. 'It's on the other side of the port.'

'The Jungle?'

'That's what it's called. It's where the Afghans sleep. It's in the dunes. There are only thorn bushes, though, there aren't really any trees.'

'Ah, the *Djangal!*' Aryan suddenly understands. The Farsi word for forest, for mayhem and disorder. He pauses, trying to think what to do.

'To get there, is it far?' he asks.

'You have to cross the whole town.'

Kabir tugs at his jacket. He is cold, and Aryan knows he can't push him to walk much further.

It is nearly dark and now that they've stopped moving Aryan is starting to shiver; their new clothes and the second-hand ones they got from a church in Paris are not going to be enough.

'Is there a place we could stay here, just for tonight?' Aryan asks. 'Tomorrow we will go away, to the Afghan camp.'

The youth hesitates, looking from him to Kabir. Aryan guesses the boy, though his build is slight, must be two or three years his elder.

'Is that a real diamond?' Kabir's eyes are wide with wonder.

The African bursts into laughter, and Aryan is astonished by the way it lights up his whole face. 'If that's a diamond then you'd be talking to the richest man in Calais!' the young man says.

At the same time, he seemed to have reached a conclusion.

'Welcome to Little Africa,' he says. 'Most of us sleep here.'

As they cross the yard the players' shoes make scuffing sounds in the sand, punctuated by the dull thwack of the ball smacking the wall. The game is moving fast, all elbows and dancing feet, and suddenly they are surrounded by it, weaving players passing and stopping and threading the ball between Aryan's shoes and bouncing it over Kabir's head, leaping around and around till all Aryan can see is a blur of colour and all he can hear is the heave of their breathing. And then, as quickly, they scatter and spread and dive and shout and groan as the ball hits home between a barrel and a blue plastic crate.

'You play?' the Somali asks.

The matches with Omar seem so long ago now that they could have been played by a different person. But in that brief contact with the ball Aryan felt the reflex rush of excitement, and longed for it again.

'I used to be a forward,' he says.

'We play to get warm before the night. We could do with another man. After that I will show you where you can bed down.'

'Thank you,' Aryan says, touching his hand to his heart before extending it. 'I am Aryan. This is my brother Kabir.'

'Jonah,' the young man says, awkwardly accepting Aryan's hand.

He turns to the players who have halted their game to stare. 'OK, Arsenal, stand by. We have just purchased Afghanistan's Ronaldinho.'

The fading smell of sump oil hits them first. Aryan remembers it from a long time ago, from the mechanics' workshop near the house they lived in when Baba was still alive, in the town in Afghanistan.

The site looks like it was once home to a swathe of old industries: a sawmill, a mechanics' workshop, a carpenters' yard. Most of the old machinery has gone, but the concrete pits remain in the cavernous warehouse whose floor is patterned with an archipelago of grease. A rusting engine base stands useless as a tree-stump. What pieces of furniture there are have come from somewhere else, incongruous amid the industrial abandon: armchairs rescued from the footpath in brown or green velour, kitchen chairs with perilous legs, like theatre props awaiting a play. Some of them have cigarette scars. In the midst of them, someone is trying to coax a campfire back to life. Along the open side of the building blankets hang across the beams in an attempt to keep out the wind.

Jonah leads them past this place to a smaller building with a pitched roof and gaps in its wooden walls. Its floor of boggy earth is mulched with orange peel and discarded clothes and the hormonal stench of urine. As if crossing a pond they walk on planks to avoid sinking into the detritus. Aryan can see no door nor any other room; before he has time to wonder, Jonah has reached the wall and is starting to climb.

Entire horizontal planks have been prised away for firewood, leaving some splintering off into the void. The shoes of previous climbers have encrusted the slats in mud. Jonah disappears into a square cut out of the ceiling before his grin reappears in its frame. Aryan sends Kabir up after him, lifting him on to the first rung. Then he clambers up himself, ducking to avoid the beams.

They emerge into another world; Aryan marvels that he has not even imagined its presence from outside. In a triangular space criss-crossed by rafters lies mattress upon mattress, blanket upon blanket, arranged in an ethereal dormitory. There are little hillocks of daypacks, and anoraks hanging off nails in the rough-hewn wood. A mound of blankets stirs and two faces peer out; Aryan is surprised to see they are girls. Like the sights in a bunker, small chinks in the wall show the outside world in stripes; the place smells of woodsmoke and damp.

Kabir's eyes widen with excitement.

'Can we sleep here too?' he asks.

'You can have this spot,' says Jonah. 'Some guys left the other day. I don't think anyone's using their sleeping bags now.'

'Thank you, we are very grateful,' Aryan says.

'I am from Somalia,' Jonah says. 'Most people here are from Somalia or Eritrea. My friend playing football is from Somalia too. Those girls are from Nigeria; there are others from Congo and Ghana and Guinea. We have all of Africa here, like the United Nations.'

'Is everybody going to England?'

Jonah laughs. 'We didn't come here for the sightseeing,' he says. 'England is my dream. England is everybody's dream. You step off the truck and they are waiting there to give you a job, no problemo.'

Aryan smiles. He has heard those stories too and wonders if they are true. Maybe people will be waiting there to take them to school.

'How long have you been here?' he asks.

'Five weeks.'

Aryan is taken aback.

'There are too many controls,' Jonah says. 'It's very hard to get through the port.'

Aryan pulls a packet of biscuits from his daypack and offers them to the Somali, but Jonah shakes his head.

'I ate earlier at the lighthouse,' he says. 'They distribute meals there every day. Tomorrow we will take you there.'

Moments later they watch the curly dome of his head disappear through the attic floor.

Aryan and Kabir divide up the biscuits, setting some aside for the morning. They pass the plastic water bottle back and forth. They still have the last of the hard bread and the cheese they have kept from Paris, and Kabir still has an apple. He eats around the bruises, turning it into a green and white asteroid. Then they venture outside to piss.

When they find their way back to the attic Kabir arranges his outermost sweater for a pillow, as Aryan has shown him. They pull the prickly blankets around them against the cold.

A drop on his eyelid shocks him from sleep. Panicked, Aryan sits up suddenly in the darkness; the cold envelops him like the blanket he has just kicked off. Above him, a patch of night sky winks down through a hole in the ceiling. He struggles through disorientation like a diver swimming up for air. Snowmelt. He shifts his bedding closer to the rafter, away from the icy dripping. He pats the wooden slats in the darkness till he finds his anorak, then folds part of it over his head. He pulls the scratchy blanket back around him. From the shadows behind him comes the sound of snoring; somebody whimpers and turns.

They are sleeping the disturbed slumber of escapees, shallow-breathed, all of them haunted by trouble of some kind.

Outside he hears a sound. A footstep crunches on gravel, then stops. In the attic there is a stiffening as wakening ears strain to listen. Again the same sound; Aryan guesses there are two people below them in the yard. All at once, as if in a collective movement, the sleepers nearest the back wall leap to their feet and scramble for the hole in the slats that leads to the adjoining roof. There is shoving, cursing, confusion, and suddenly the whizz of a missile shooting up through the gap in the floor. The canister hits the rafters and lands on a pile of bedding. Someone kicks it away; it fizzes like a crazy bird with a vaporous plume. Those who haven't woken in time bury themselves under the covers; fighting off the blanket that has become entangled in his feet Aryan reaches for his shoes. Kabir is already doing the same. There is a smaller hole beside the big one and the last thing Aryan sees is Kabir shoving himself through it on to the roof.

Suddenly Aryan's eyes are streaming. He trips on a sleeping bag and lands on the floor. It feels like his eyes are bleeding. Needles of pain shoot to the back of his sockets, stinging and burning like acid. He tries to open his eyelids, but light and toxic fire sear his streaming eyeballs. He hears swearing and the clatter of feet on the fibreglass roof. His heart is pounding and he is breathing fast and tears pour from his blinded eyes. Through his panic he can hear the stuttering of a police radio, the click-clack of reloading, and boots making their way across the railyard to the old mechanics' workshop where the others are still asleep. In the yard outside, the sound of shouts and running feet.

Through the hot liquid of his eyes, chinks of light began to appear, and a blurred kaleidoscope of colour. But there is sand inside his eyelids and keeping them shut is the only way to hold the pain at bay. His head throbs. It reminds him of the time when, long ago, he had been playing with chilli peppers in the kitchen and had rubbed his fists in his eyes. Sight had vanished then, and he had yelled to decapitate the mountains before it returned.

'Here, take this,' a low voice says. A plastic bottle is thrust into his hands. 'Cup your hand and splash this on your eyes.'

The acrid smell still hangs in the air but Aryan does as the voice advises. Someone takes the bottle from him and pours more water on to his hands, and he washes his eyeballs as best he can. The more he rubs, the more it stings. His eyes feel like an ocean weeping endless water; he is maddened with blindness and fright.

'Keep rinsing,' comes the voice like a guardian angel's. 'The water will wash the tear-gas out.'

He cups his hand and bathes his right eye, then his left, then the right again, until slowly the stinging starts to abate.

'Kabir!' he bellows. In his pain he has forgotten he is not by his side.

'Here, Aryan.' The voice is a small distance away, beyond the rafters, outside.

Gradually the world returns – lozenges of colour, and shadow, and pencils of piercing light.

Mounds become backpacks, triangles become rafters, verticals become people again. Swirling shapes turn back into mounds of bedding. The splashes of brightness become chinks in the wall where the dawn is squinting through.

'Can you see anything yet?' the voice says.

'Almost,' Aryan says. He feels nauseous with the stench of gas and the aftertaste of fear.

At last he can make out his brother, bottle in hand, red eyes streaming too.

'They do this just about every day,' the angel says. Through tear-blur Aryan makes out the form of a skinny Somali boy with a narrow face and corkscrew hair. 'Keep a bottle of water where you sleep. There's a tap next door. Next time you will know what to do.'

Relief mingles with shock that this could happen. Aryan doesn't understand. This is not a country at war; in Europe they are meant to be safe.

'Who is attacking us?' he asks.

'It's the police,' the boy says.

'Why would the police attack us?'

'Because they don't want us here.'

'We don't want to stay either.'

'Nobody does. Everybody is trying to leave.'

'Then what is the point of attacking us?'

The boy shrugs. 'They have special police to control us. They bring new ones every month so they're always fresh. It's just the way it is.'

Aryan feels like he is losing his footing. He doesn't understand how they could have become a target. They are not warriors and they don't have weapons – they are on the run from those very things. It is as if the police in France have been given the wrong information, and have been sent in to attack the wrong side.

The plastic bottle twists in the fire like molten glass. As the water inside it slowly heats, it sways and beckons like a belly dancer, releasing invisible fumes.

On one side of the cavernous machine hall, an angular Eritrean sits in the largest armchair – all green velvet and sawn-off legs – drinking tea from the sole china cup. Standing, or seated on crates and wobbly benches beside him, the others pass around plastic beakers to share. The Eritrean's limbs are too big for the chair – his bent knees stand higher than his waist. A peaked cap shades triangular cheekbones and sharp, light eyes. There is an aura about him – Aryan can't quite place it – in the coldness of his gaze, in the careful formality with which he is treated by the other youths.

Slowly the circle widens as more Africans emerge from their sleeping places. They hug their hands under their armpits, rub their eyes, rinse out the last of the tear-gas with water from plastic bottles, calm now after the alarm of dawn.

Aryan and Kabir hesitate a little way from the circle until Jonah gestures to them, diamond earring twinkling. The bottom of his red football shirt is hanging below a jacket, a sweatshirt and two sweaters. The other Africans eye them curiously until Jonah says something to them in their language and they relax, and shuffle sideways to open a space. Aryan declines the offer of a packing-crate seat.

The slow-dancing bottle shares the fire with an enamel cooking pot half-filled with water, tea-bags dangling from its edge. Inside, ash particles circle like microscopic fish; a torn cardboard box of sugar-cubes sits nearly empty on the ground. Kabir squats, and plays with a piece of plywood he has edged into the coals. Aryan feels the warmth put colour in his face, and turns his back to the flames when the smoke sidles his way. It reminds him of the cooking fires at home, his mother stoking the wood stove in their kitchen of hardened earth. Quickly he bats the thought away.

One of the Somalis leans forward in his rickety chair, playing a pop song on the speaker of his mobile phone. 'Bye-bye-bye,' the crackly voice sings to his girlfriend. 'Please don't say it's bye-bye-bye.' His neighbours sing along in low voices as they wait for the water to boil.

Beside the pot, very slowly, the plastic bottle flexes and contorts as its transparent ribs cloud in the heat. To Aryan it seems a miracle that it can still stand upright, the cool water inside stopping it from subsiding into a petrochemical pool. He wonders if the fumes are poisonous. A young man with a shark's tooth around his neck steadies it with a pair of sticks, watching for steam. Then his friend, in a white hooded sweatshirt and hair grown wild from weeks on the road, grips it with his T-shirt and lifts it gently from the coals.

Circumventing the patches where snow was dripping from the roof, they carry it to the centre of the room where mechanics once worked, and stand over a hole in the floor filled with grease and discarded clothes.

It is bitterly cold, and conversation curls from their mouths in indecipherable comic-strip swirls.

'You go first,' says the one with the shark's tooth round his neck.

Opposite the fire, and its ring of packing crates and broken armchairs, the walls are rimmed with bedding, daypacks and shoes. Like a man on a stage, the youth stands there in a T-shirt, rubbing a bar of soap between his hands.

Then he cranes his neck, and his friend pours the warm water over the crown of his head, and the whorls of his hair turn white as a Grecian statue as the lather takes hold. He scrubs, and his friend rinses, and afterwards he shakes his head like a puppy and rubs it dry with his T-shirt. Then he does the same for his friend, bare-chested, shark's tooth gleaming just below the indentation of his throat. Afterwards, the two of them come back to dry off by the fire.

Moments later, in the freezing space of the cavernous

shelter swept night and day by the wind, laughter echoes from the concrete walls and up to the dripping rafters.

'Hagos, your hair's on fire!'

The boys look at each other and grin. From their warm, damp heads clouds of steam unfurl as thick as halos in the icy air. They hop about flapping their hands, pretending to pat out invisible flames. In this, their bathroom-bedroom-living-room filled with rubbish and rat bait and grease, they clown around, almost normal, almost relaxed, almost teenagers again, as the steam rises and their hair dries and their skin grows taut from the soap and the cleanness and the warmth.

Aryan joins in the laughter too. It feels like an eternity since he has surrendered to the compulsive joy of it. He laughs till the tears come to his eyes, surprised he has any tears left, with relief and a sort of involuntary release. He has held so much in check for so long. Kabir is giggling his Kabir giggle, black eyes shining above luminous cheeks. Jonah nearly falls backwards off his packing crate. For a moment Aryan forgets his hunger and his tiredness and everything they have been through just to get to this place, sheltering like derelicts in the rafters at the back of a rail-way yard in the icy European winter. He forgets the stomach-cramps that pierce his sleep and the fizzing of tear-gas canisters. He forgets how far they are from home, and how alone they are, and how unfit he feels for this journey, and how there is no going back.

He lets the spasms wash over him until they are spent.

When the water in the enamel pot starts bubbling, one of the Africans slides it off the fire and ladles the brown liquid into plastic cups thrust towards him in outstretched hands.

Kabir is sitting next to a teenager in a Bob Marley T-shirt who is rocking backwards on a loose-jointed chair. He slides a piece of wire as thick as a bucket handle into the fire and leaves it there, checking its colour and pushing it in deeper and turning it until the length of it glows as red as a neon sign.

Then, calmly, while his friends sip their tea, he withdraws it from the coals and, in a single gesture, closes his fingers over it and pulls it through.

Mouth agape, Kabir scans his face for pain.

The youth opens his hand to examine the effect. Kabir kneels up to look. A polished line runs across skin turned yellow with scar tissue.

'Does it hurt?' Kabir says.

The teenager shakes his head. 'It's for the fingerprints,' he says. 'So they can't send me back.'

Under an oppressive sky they traipse along a disused railway line towards the port. Jonah walks ahead of them with some of the Somalis Aryan recognizes from last night's game. His feet are ice and he feels light-headed with hunger. The tracks lead them along a murky canal and then veer off, running parallel to a road. Ahead, Jonah ducks under the barbed wire, and Aryan and Kabir follow suit.

They emerge on the edge of a car park squeezed between the railroad track and the canal. Aryan falters. Spread out before them, beside a temporary cabin and a row of green rubbish bins, they see scores and scores of men, queuing, leaning on the fences, sitting on the street kerb, picnicking in small groups on the ground between the puddles in the patchy asphalt. They sit hunched against the cold in dark anoraks and knitted hats – the camouflage of the unauthorized, the phantom men on the road.

'Ravens,' Kabir says. 'They look like lots of birds.'

A car is parked beside the cabin, its four doors open wide like a beetle's wings. Music pours from the speakers. Africans are sitting everywhere: inside, on the bonnet, in the boot, hanging on the doors. The car rocks on its suspension with the beat.

Jonah makes a detour to high-five them as he heads to the queue.

In low gear a police car cruises by, windows sealed, invisible eyes watching behind the reflections. Nobody runs.

Aryan takes a step backwards. There must be more than three hundred men gathered there under the metallic clouds. He had no idea they were so many.

Jonah turns back to look for them, taking a moment to locate them on the edge of the crowd.

'Come on!' he calls. 'There'll be none left if you wait.'

There are big groups of Africans in one queue – Nigerians, Somalis and Eritreans – alternating with Afghani Pashtuns and knots of Tajiks and a big group of

173

Hazaras. Further on there are Kurds and Iraqis and Iranians and Pakistanis, everyone babbling in different languages. There is a Kurdish youth on crutches with one leg missing below the knee. Aryan and Kabir join the shortest line.

Aryan turns to the man behind them. He has ears like handles and a wide friendly face and a gap between his front teeth.

'*Salaam alaikum*,' Aryan says.

The man returns his greeting. 'Are you new around here?' he says. 'I'd have remembered the boy.'

'We got here last night,' Aryan says. 'We are looking for the Afghan camp.'

'You know someone there?' The man's friends bunch around them in the queue to listen.

'No. My brother and I need somewhere to stay for just a couple of days, before we go to England.'

The man guffaws. 'Just a couple of days!'

His friends join in the laughter.

Aryan flushes with confusion.

'You might need more than a few days, my friend,' the man says. 'You will see. But you can stay at the Kabul Hilton while you're waiting.'

'Where?' Aryan looks puzzled.

'Five stars,' the man says. 'Hot water, feather pillows – you'll never want to leave.'

The men grin and pick up the baton.

'Room service for breakfast! How do you like your eggs?' says one.

'Same-day laundry service! Kindly place your socks in the bag!' says another.

'The shoeshine service is free! Just leave your boots outside the door!'

Aryan shrinks with embarrassment. Men ahead of them and behind them are chiming in.

'One hundred television channels, and all the movies you want!'

'Fresh towels for the swimming pool!'

'And heated towels for your bath!'

'And if you feel like doing some sightseeing, sign up for our Jungle Tours!'

Kabir's black eyes are alight. 'Can we go there, Aryan?' he says.

The men fall about laughing.

'They're only joking, Kabir,' Aryan says.

'Kabul Hilton – it's what we call the Jungle, my friend,' says the man with the handle ears. 'It's where all the Afghans stay.'

'Is there room for two more?' Aryan asks.

'Sure, my friend. You can come with us.'

'Why do they call it the Jungle?' Kabir says.

'It's not really a jungle,' the man says. 'It's just a derelict place full of thorns.'

They are near the head of the queue. Steam rises from giant cauldrons. A Frenchwoman doles couscous into white polystyrene trays; another, cheeks glistening from the vapour, ladles out vegetable broth. A man hands them chunks of

175

that weightless bread, and a plastic bag with forks, apples, yoghurt, chocolate, and sometimes a cigarette.

Two Frenchmen patrol the lines, dousing scuffles, weeding out queue-hoppers, protecting the trestle tables from any shoving.

Suddenly there is a pop-pop sound. A car accelerates; a burly Iraqi clutches his shoulder and yells. From the ground at his feet he picks up the pellet from an air rifle. The car has already disappeared.

The woman who hands Kabir his tray smiles and says 'bonjour' and gives him an extra bar of chocolate. Her face is a collection of right-angles framed by frizzy hair.

Aryan cannot eat apples. He gives his piece of fruit away.

Kabir walks carefully, pursing his lips in concentration as he balances his plastic tray, watching his feet. His too-long trousers drag on the ground. The plastic bag swings from his wrist like a pendulum, gathering speed. He stops to break its velocity.

'Over here,' says the man from the queue, beckoning them to where he sits in a small circle on the edge of the canal.

Ravenously, they eat. Their first hot food in days, it fills them and glues to their insides.

'I am Khaled,' the man says, wiping a hand on his trousers and holding it out.

'I am Aryan. This is Kabir, my brother.'

The man releases his grip.

'Is everyone here going to England?' Aryan asks, impressed by the crowd.

'Trying to,' Khaled says. 'As you'll find, it's not that easy.'

'How long have you been here?'

'Nine weeks.'

Aryan starts. That was even longer than Jonah. Surely it only took a few days?

'Who've you been listening to?' Khaled says. 'My friend has been here eleven weeks, some people have been here three months. It's very hard to get across. The port is crawling with police.'

The men must be doing something wrong, Aryan thinks. England is very close. Thirty kilometres away. He saw it on the map the Afghan with the zippers showed him back in Paris, one afternoon by the canal.

A man on the edge of the circle is concentrating so hard on something in his hand that he doesn't immediately notice Kabir's stare.

A flash of silver. Kabir nudges Aryan. It takes him a moment to realize the man is carving at his fingertips with a razor blade.

Music still throbs from the African car. Aryan has lost Jonah in the crowd.

They line up for tea. It is served from a window in the cabin whose outside walls are covered in graffiti in all languages: Arabic, Pashto, Farsi, Urdu, Kurdish, English, and others that Aryan can't recognize. There are felt-tip pictures of houses. Names. Cryptic messages scribbled in blue ink. Ways of trying to remember; a noticeboard for those following behind.

The tea is hot and black and sweet. They hold the flimsy cups by the rim and blow on them, trying not to burn their fingers.

Aryan is looking for his language on the cabin walls. Then he finds it.

'Never Never Never give up,' he reads, in red, indelible ink.

Kabir trots behind Khaled. Aryan follows behind looking for landmarks, trying to memorize the way.

The town is a labyrinth. Streets peter out in dead ends. Motorways circle, double back, intersect, fly over bridges, ring traffic islands, lie parallel yet inaccessible to each other behind walls of bisecting wire.

Beside the port, trucks grind past in all directions in a choreography of primary colours.

'I like the yellow ones best,' Kabir says.

'Why's that?' says Aryan.

'Yellow makes me happy,' he says. 'It's the colour of the sun.'

'I thought red was your favourite colour this week, because of Jonah's shirt.'

'Well I like red too,' Kabir says. 'I think I like them both.'

Aryan laughs. 'Maybe you should settle for orange,' he says.

They stop on the edge of the port and peer through the boundary fence. They see ramps, cranes, and prefabricated offices piled on top of each other like children's blocks. Trucks wait in long rows in the parking bay. Drivers cluster between the semi-trailers to smoke, waiting for a man in a fluorescent jacket to wave their vehicles through.

The ferryboats gorge on a slow-moving procession of cargo trucks that fills them with colourful cubes.

At the edge of the last parking bay, asphalt gives way to sand. On the far side of a double strip of motorway, the steel and concrete stacks of a factory rear out of the industrial flatness. The biggest chimney has red-and-white stripes like an oversized barber's pole. TIOXIDE is emblazoned in giant letters across the side.

'Chemicals,' Khaled says. 'Keep right away from there.'

He leads them down a narrow track between bushes that stand as high as a man. They bend low to avoid the thorns that snag their clothes as they wind through twisting paths, and emerge into a small clearing. At the centre of it lie the remains of a campfire. Three packing-crate huts are tucked around its edges like sagging igloos roofed with pastel blankets. The place is strewn with rubbish: sodden paper, rotting fruit and plastic bottles decorate the undergrowth. An old T-shirt and a discarded shoe lie abandoned in the dirt; someone has draped a pair of trousers over the bushes hoping to dry them in the damp sea air. The picture of a rat flickers across Aryan's brain.

'This one is empty,' says Khaled, indicating one of the huts. 'It might need a few repairs, but no one is staying there now.'

'Thank you,' Aryan says.

'Like we were saying, the Kabul Hilton,' Khaled says.

But Kabir is already scrambling inside. He lets out a whoop.

'Look, Aryan!' he says.

He emerges backwards, on his knees, with something unwieldy in his hands. Outside, he raises it to the sky. A cage, and inside it, a canary. There is a bell made of seeds, and a swinging perch.

'Don't touch him, Kabir,' Aryan says. 'He'll have germs.'

But Kabir's hand is already in the cage, stroking the yellow feathers, the speckled wings.

'I can feel his heart beating!' Kabir says.

'That's generally a good sign,' says Khaled.

Aryan remembers the homing pigeons his grandfather used to keep on the roof of their house in Afghanistan, how they would circle the baked city, their wings white against the stony backdrop of mountains as the heat drained out of the day. The old man would feed one with a piece of bread and hold its feet so that it flapped its wings, and the rest of the flock would hear it no matter how high up they were or where they were over the valley. In a clapping and flapping and beating of whiteness that at first made Aryan afraid, they would all come in to land in a flurry of beaks and feathers and strange orange eyes and claws. He remembers them from before Kabir was born, before they went to Iran, before they didn't have pigeons any more.

'Don't worry, he can't fly,' Khaled says. 'His tail feathers were probably stolen by the police.'

Kabir is kicking through the rubbish hunting for something he can use for water. He whistles at the bird through the bars of the cage.

'He's lost his voice, too,' Khaled says. 'But you can have him if you want. Maybe you can get him to remember some tunes.'

Khaled has kicked over the old ashes and is building a small pyramid of paper and twigs in order to make a new fire.

'Did they make it to England?' Aryan asks.

'Who?' Khaled says.

'The guys who slept here before. The ones who left the canary.'

'Yes, though it took them a few weeks.'

'How many weeks?' says Aryan.

'I didn't count. But it must have been five or six.'

Six weeks. Aryan swallows. He is worried how long their money will last, about how much more they will need.

'Some guys have been trying for a lot longer.'

'How do you know they got across?'

'We know because Idris told us.'

'Who is Idris?'

Khaled laughs. 'Everyone knows Idris. You'll meet him soon enough. He is the guy who organizes the trucks. He knows everything that goes on. People phone him when they get to the other side. Or they phone their friends and they tell him. You can't go anywhere without him – not even for a piss half the time.'

They are inside the hut, and Kabir has snuggled close to his brother for warmth. He smells faintly of sweat and the sticky sea air. The blankets are musty with old dirt. Aryan thinks about fleas, about the bites they got in Greece, remembers how sick they were there.

'Can we get some super glue?' Kabir says after a while.

Aryan wonders if he has heard correctly. 'Super glue?'

'To hide our fingerprints. Khaled said we can get it from the store.'

'We don't need to hide our fingerprints – we haven't been fingerprinted anywhere.'

'But if the French police catch us, Khaled says they will fingerprint us. Khaled says that means they will send us back here if they find us in England.'

'Let's talk about it tomorrow. Get some sleep, Kabir.'

Kabir is silent for a while. Then:

'Aryan?'

'What, Kabir?'

'Did you hear that sound?'

'What sound?'

'That rustling sound. Like someone in the bushes.'

'No. You're imagining things. Go to sleep.'

'There are ghosts out there, Aryan.'

'Says who?'

'The Afghans round the campfire. Some of the boys were talking about them.'

'Well you should block your ears. They are only trying to scare you.'

'They said there were killer ghosts that came out at night with knives. They said one man got attacked.'

'More likely he got in a fight,' Aryan says. 'Those ghosts are all in their heads.'

'They said there was lots of blood. The ghosts were filthy with matted hair. They said they were the guards of the Jungle and they flashed their knives and said they would take revenge on trespassers, no matter who they were.'

Aryan shivers. Kabir's ghosts remind him of the ones that terrified him as a child: malodorous creatures with ragged beards who rained rocks down from the mountainsides, guarding the pass behind the village where Baba was from. His earliest memories of fear. Immediately he smothers the thought.

'Kabir,' he says. 'It's only a story. It's something invented by the smugglers to protect their terrain.'

'I'm scared, Aryan.'

'Why would you be scared of ghosts? You were brave when we crossed the river into Greece. You were brave when we ran away from the farm. You were brave in the desert and when we crossed over the mountains with the horsemen. You can't tell me that now you're spooked by a story some guys have made up.'

'Sometimes I think about that man on the farm. Maybe he is trying to get me.'

Aryan catches his breath. 'That man is a long way away, Kabir,' he says. 'He can't find you here. Even if he knew you were here, which he doesn't. Even if he were out looking for you, which he isn't.'

'How do you know? Maybe they are angry with us for running away.'

'We are the ones who should be angry with them. They didn't pay us, remember. And they didn't help us go to Italy like they said.'

'He could come in his truck.'

'Even if he did, he'd have better things to do than look for you.'

'He might want to take us back.'

'They've probably got other boys working there now. You're only scared because it's dark. I bet you aren't frightened during the day.'

'Sometimes I am. Sometimes I think I see him.'

'You see him? Where?'

'In the town. Near the lighthouse where we get food. Sometimes near the Jungle.'

It is only now Aryan realizes that Kabir is trembling.

'It's your imagination, Kabir. That man is not here, believe me. He is a thousand miles away. Next time you think you see him, tell me, and I'll prove you wrong, I swear it. And next time you hear those ghost stories, put your hands over your ears, like this.'

Kabir doesn't say anything.

'Do you think you will be able to sleep now?' Aryan says.

'I don't know.'

'Do you remember the English words I taught you?'

'Some of them,' Kabir says.

'And the counting?'

'Yes, I remember that.'

'So count to twenty in English and then start again. Baba always used to say you can't count and be scared at the same time.'

Something startles him awake.

Rigid, Aryan scans the blackness with eyes that refuse to see. He can't identify the sound that has wrenched him back to consciousness. He lifts his head in the darkness, every sense alert. He hears Kabir's steady breathing somewhere beside him under the blankets that were heavy without being warm. The stale stench of socks and bedding fills his nostrils; a wan light thins the sides of the hut where it penetrates the plastic sheeting like a membrane. Overhead all is dark; the blankets that make up the roof have blocked out the sky. In the distance he can hear the sea. He shifts his body softly, easing the pressure where the slats of the packing crates were digging in to his bones, his brain still searching.

Suddenly, it's there again: the crackle of a short-wave radio. Like a stab of lightning the noise throws him back to the house in Afghanistan where the sound of electronic voices was the prelude to danger. There is a sour taste in his mouth and one blind thought in his head: escape.

Aryan grabs Kabir, thrusts a hand over his mouth and leans into his ear. 'Get your shoes,' he says.

Kabir jack-knifes awake. He crawls out of his blankets with neither cry nor complaint. Aryan feels in the dark-ness of the hut for his own trainers, shoves in his feet, turns to Kabir who is fumbling in the tangle of bedclothes.

'I can't find them.' There is panic in Kabir's voice.

Aryan flails about under the piles of bedding tossed into the hut by others who had nested there before them; Kabir's shoes are nowhere to be found. 'Get on my back,' he says.

He can hear the radio-crackle getting nearer – then a shout as the police reach another hut in the thorn bushes and the men caught sleeping inside it start to protest. Kabir lassoes Aryan's neck with his arms, threads his legs through his elbows.

'Keep your head down,' Aryan says, as he crawls through the blanket flap and out into the clear night air.

'Hey, you!' a voice cries in English. 'Police! Stop now!'

Aryan bolts.

There is a sound of thrashing behind him, as if someone is slashing the vegetation. Aryan can't tell if the shouts are directed at them or at somebody else.

Then another voice, that seems to come from the hut next to theirs. 'I got one! Here, quick!'

There is only one way out through the bushes and Aryan takes it. Branches tear at his face and shirt as he hurls himself, half strangled by the child on his back, along the sandy path that winds like a rabbit track through the warren of thorns.

'Shut your eyes,' he says. He is bent double as the barbs rip at cloth and skin.

There is just enough light in the pre-dawn sky to make out the track, and where it forks he takes the branch that leads away from the truck park, away from the port, down through the spinifex dunes to the sea. His feet kick dry footprints in the sand's damp crust. His heart is thumping; Kabir's breath is hot on the nape of his neck; round arms are putting pressure on his windpipe. Aryan clutches at them as his legs work underneath him, under Kabir's dragging weight. His chest heaves with the effort, with the subsidence under his feet as the sand deepens on the trail.

Behind them he can hear shouts, and the barking of dogs, as men exhausted by the night's fruitless efforts to conceal themselves on freight trucks are wrenched from shallow slumber by the raid.

When they reach the edge of the dunes, the wind that picks up just before sunrise hits them full in the face. Aryan turns his head sideways to listen. No police dogs, no army boots pound behind them; no one, it seems, has given chase. He sets Kabir down on the sand and grips him by the wrist.

'Come on,' he says between painful breaths. 'We'll be safer just a bit further along.'

'It's cold,' Kabir says, his socks sinking into the sand. The breeze is coming at them straight off the sea.

'Keep moving, Spiderman, then you won't notice.'

A few metres around the base of the dune Aryan flings himself down on his back and waits for the pounding in his chest to subside.

After a while he turns his head to look sideways at Kabir. 'You OK?' he asks.

Small pearls of blood well along a scratch above his eye. 'Yes, OK,' he says.

They sit in silence. Kabir makes moon craters in the sand, quarrying through the damp surface to the fine dry particles beneath.

When did Kabir stop being a little boy? Aryan wonders. It is not just that his brother is nearly too heavy for him now, not just that his own voice is starting to break. They are both growing up on the road.

It feels like they have been travelling for ever. Now that England is suddenly so much closer, he realizes how little he really knows, how little he can even imagine of what things will be like when they arrive.

Aryan sits up. The wind parts his hair, already grown thick since the last time it was cut, by Rahim's wife in Rome.

'Look, over there,' he says. 'That's England.'

It has been a clear night, and dawn is starting to smear the horizon pink. A tanker slides between the marker buoys and the early ferries approach, merge and separate on an aluminium sea. A string of lights winks on the opposite shore, beyond a diaphanous outline of cliffs.

'It doesn't look so far,' Kabir says.

'I know,' Aryan says. 'It's only thirty kilometres. But it's further than it seems.'

He thinks about how far they have travelled, and how strange it is that the hardest part of their journey should come at the end.

'They say the police in England don't carry any guns,' Aryan says.

Kabir is quiet, trying to imagine that. 'Maybe they don't have any bad guys,' he says.

'Or maybe the police outsmart them.'

Dry strands of seaweed skim the beach, hissing and tangling with driftwood and stray pieces of orange rope. A plastic bottle rolls in demented circles. Kabir covers his eyes to keep out the sand.

'Why did the police come to the camp?' he asks.

'It's because they don't want us here.'

'We don't want to be here either,' Kabir says. 'They should just let us go on the boat.'

'You can if you've got a passport and a visa and a ticket,' Aryan says.

'Why don't we just get them?'

'Don't I wish we could.'

A flock of gulls chases the SeaFrance ferry out to sea.

'How long do you think it's going to take to get there?' Kabir says.

'Who knows,' Aryan says. 'We have to find out how things work. Then after that, we'll just need a bit of luck.'

Aryan lies back in the sand. He can feel the cold grit of it funnelling down the back of his T-shirt and filling his shoes, but suddenly he is too tired to care. It is enough just to get himself and Kabir through each day. He looks up at the stars that are fading in the watery dawn and thinks of the stars where he was born, passive overseers of so much strife, and wonders how long they will have to bear this limbo, suspended between a past they can no longer return to, and a future that's taking for ever to unfurl.

'Hamid!'

Kabir's high-pitched shout makes half the men in the food queue spin around.

With all the power in his short legs he hurtles down the line, nearly tripping over his laces and the flaps of his jeans, and barrels into Hamid's ribs with the full force of his eight-year-old body.

There is a driving rain and it is already dark. Hungry men in five layers of clothes hunch inside their anoraks like monks hoping for alms. Their faces are sombre inside their hoods.

'Hamid! You're here!'

Reeling with disbelief, Hamid prises the limpet-hands off his legs. 'Kabir!' he says, staggering backwards through his own laughter. 'Where's Aryan? Are you both here?'

But Aryan is already throwing his arms around his friend. It's been more than eight months since he last saw him in the back of the truck when it abandoned them on the farm in Greece. He feels his whole body open in a smile, doesn't care that they've lost their place in the line.

'It's really you!' Aryan says, draping his arm over Hamid's shoulder in the old gesture of friendship.

Kabir is so excited he starts to dance in the rain.

Hamid still looks the same – a little drawn perhaps, a few tiredness lines around his eyes. But there is something different about him too, Aryan thinks. Something elusive, a sort of edginess that makes him seem older than his fifteen years.

Then, he thinks, he too must have changed. They have all been through so many things.

In Aryan and Kabir's shelter, rain beating on plastic like an orchestra of drums, they wrap the stiff blankets around themselves and talk. The canary eavesdrops in the corner, enveloped in a pink rug of its own.

Hamid has been in Calais for four weeks, trying on his own to get on to the trucks.

'It's impossible,' he says. 'When you are alone there is no one to close the doors behind you, so you have to go with a friend. But no one wants to stay behind. There is no way out unless you go with a smuggler, and even then it's not sure. A lot of the guys are giving up and trying to go further north.'

'North?' Aryan says.

'They try from Belgium, or they give up on England altogether and head for Sweden, or Norway, or Denmark. Up there with the Vikings, in all that snow.'

'What about you? Are you still going to England?' Aryan asks.

'That's the plan. It's the only language in Europe I know,' he says. 'Plus that's where I have a cousin who will help me. But if it takes much longer I'm going to be too old to go to school.'

Kabir wants to know everything that's happened to Hamid since they heard him pounding on the inside of their truck.

'It's a long story,' Hamid says.

'Don't worry,' Aryan says. 'It's not like we don't have time.'

In the dimness they sit cross-legged, knee to knee, three dark pyramids of blankets.

'We were thirteen in the lorry after they dropped you two off,' Hamid begins. 'We drove for hours, and in the end the driver ditched us a long way outside Patras, sometime in the middle of the night. We walked for miles till we found the camp.'

He tells them of the scenes he remembers: men silhouetted against the glow of the campfires, or fanning their embers in the smoky dawn to bake sheets of bread over old tin petrol drums. He shows them the marks on his body: the indents from truncheon blows; the traces of police boots on his ribs; the teeth he chipped when he fell on to the road from a lorry. He tells of the shock that swept through the camp when an Afghan he knew by sight was crushed under the wheels of a truck.

Twice he made it to Italy, paying his way by working as a door-opener for a smuggler; twice the Italians returned him on the very same ferryboat to Greece. On his second crossing he was stranded at sea, hidden inside a wardrobe in the back of a furniture van, for three days when the ferry broke down; he spent two hours massaging his legs before he could walk.

'There was a rumour that kept going around the camp – and the harder things got, the more the rumour took hold – that Canada was going to send a big ship to rescue all the Afghans,' Hamid says. 'Some of the guys believed it – I did too at first. Imagine that – one big ship like Noah's ark to take us all to Canada! It took some of them ages to realize that no boat was ever going to come.'

The trucks became everyone's obsession. 'You can't imagine the knowledge we had,' Hamid says. He learned to distinguish those that were going to Italy from those that were Africa-bound. He knew that the long-distance lorries were always the last through the port.

He was in despair the second time the Italians sent him back. The Greeks took his fingerprints and stole his money and sent him to a jail with a hundred men and kept him there for forty-seven days.

Then, one night, they drove him back to the Evros. 'We thought they were going to drown us and toss our bodies downstream,' Hamid says. Instead, two dozen of them were ordered on to a boat and pushed across the river into Turkey.

He survived on moss, and the bark of trees, and last year's rice that he scrounged from the paddies along the waterway. He made his way back to the smugglers' house and argued with the father of the handicapped boy until he agreed to get him back into Greece.

This time he avoided Patras altogether. He worked as a fruit picker, then lost time in Athens, then managed to cross Europe clinging to the chassis of lorries. He ate in the kiosks at service stations, and always tried to head west.

'I don't know which countries I was in, and I lost count of the days,' Hamid says. He went through tunnels, and over mountains, and down endless corridors of highway, eyes streaming, pebbles flying, fingers so brittle that he feared he'd fall off and die like a dog on the motorway, run over by the semi-trailers following behind.

Disoriented, and aching with cramp, he made it to a city called Lyon, and locked himself in the toilet of a train till it halted at the terminus in Paris.

'There, I found the other Afghans, and slept beside the canal and sometimes in the park and sometimes under the bridges and sometimes in the underage camp inside the metro,' he says.

'We went there!' Kabir says. 'They had drawings on the walls and you could feel the vibrations of the trains in the tunnels at night.'

'That's the place,' Hamid says.

Some of the Afghans he met in Paris urged him to take the bus with them to Sweden, or to continue on to Finland, but his goal was always England. He fell in with four teen-agers camped by the canal and together they came to Calais.

'We've been here for four weeks but this place is worse than Patras,' he says. 'No place has been tougher than here.'

Aryan is startled. 'What makes you say that?' he says.

'You'll see,' says Hamid. 'It's nearly impossible to get out. Calais is a prison with invisible walls.'

'People tunnel out of prisons,' Aryan says. 'What about the tunnel that goes under the sea?'

'Everyone says it's too difficult. Some guys had a go at the fences with wire cutters and in five minutes they were surrounded by police.'

'I don't understand anything here,' Aryan says. 'We don't want to stay in France, so why don't the French just let us go?'

'Who knows?' Hamid says. 'Maybe they have some agreement with England. Maybe the English are making the French keep us out.'

'But the English sent soldiers with the Americans – they know what it's like in Afghanistan,' Aryan says. 'They are good people and everyone knows they have human rights over there.'

Hamid shrugs. 'Try telling that to the French police.'

The silence pools between them, each lost in their separate thoughts.

'You know, I'd better get back,' Hamid says after a while. 'I'm in a shelter with Farzad – he's a Tajik I met in Paris – but someone he knows from Patras is coming here this week. Maybe I could move in with you two when he does.'

Aryan smiles at him in the darkness. With Hamid around he is sure they will find a way across. For today it is enough just to have been given back his friend.

'What do you think, Kabir?' Aryan says. 'Will we let him in?'

'Hang on a moment,' says Kabir. 'I've got to check first with the canary.'

After midnight the runners come.

Tributaries of men fall in behind them. Together they weave fugitive paths through thorn bushes and under clover-leaf bypasses, their shadows bleached orange in the glow of the city at night.

Soft-footed, dark-clothed, they slip between the slumbering hulks of semi-trailers that are positioned like tanks in the car park bordering the camp and the port and the sea. Their faces are sunk deep in the hoods of their anoraks; like white birds roosting, their feet nestle beside giant tyres as they fold themselves into their own shadows.

Up ahead, the runner tries the seals and locks. When they won't give he moves on to the next and the next.

Finally he scales a tyre and peers into the cabin, scanning the dashboard for route records and telltale debris from the road. Then he darts to the back of the truck. Cargo-laden, it's headed for England. He saws at the hard plastic seal with a pocket-knife and swings open the doors.

Quickly they clamber in, blood beating loudly in their ears. This time. This time. All of them are scared. Some are jumpy, some are calm, some trip and lose their footing, some are desperate, some are almost paralysed with fear. Some draw courage from the danger. Others curse or jostle or are nauseous at the demons of the night: violence, claustrophobia, police. Some are taunted by the devils at their back, by complicated debts involving land or their sisters or their homes. Others fear suffocation, or that their pounding hearts will seize up or give way or give them away; others still fear beatings by the drivers or the police. In the great lottery of their journeys all of them are survivors, but tonight only a few will pass this test.

For the others, a squalid dawn will reveal the bedraggled bounty of failure: police vans disgorging new candidates for detention; databases whirring through a million finger-prints in search of a match; the red-eyed, damp-footed night-walkers waking to disappointment at finding them-selves still here, still prisoners, still hostage to Calais's leaden skies.

'The mid-week nights are best,' the man is saying. There is no sunshine, but his eyes are hidden behind mirrored sunglasses in which Aryan can see nothing but a gnome-like version of himself awash in a petroleum sheen. 'Tuesday, Wednesday, Thursday. Those are the busiest days in the port, so your odds are going to be better for getting through.'

Nobody knows his full name. The Afghans all call him Idris, but no one ever addresses him directly. He is always wearing the same clothes – the only man in white mole-skin trousers and leather boots that set him apart both from the Afghans he is constantly circling and from the runners who guide them to the trucks. Idris has people to do that for him now. Some say he is from Morocco, others, a Kurd; he speaks Pashto, and Farsi, as well as Arabic and the language of the Kurds. At twilight he emerges from no one knows where to cruise the camps in a sort of recruitment drive, ingratiating himself with the new arrivals, staking out his territory, joking while obliging them to sign up. Once they do, they become his property and his clan.

If the Afghans respect him they also keep their distance; it is always Idris who suddenly appears among them, jovial but quietly menacing, clocking their moves with an attentive eye. It is not the year-round suntan so much as the swagger that sets him apart; less the ruby on his finger than the miraculously laundered clothes that suggest his power, and the boots with the Cuban heels that prove he never has to run. In his presence Aryan feels grubby, self-conscious, like merchandise of inferior weft.

'You can still try your luck on the covered trucks but you know it's riskier now that they've doubled the detectors,' Idris is saying.

There is murmuring among the knot of men gathered under the peeling lighthouse. Aryan thinks of it alternately with affection and suspicion, a landmark but also an echo chamber that hoards their secrets in its caracole insides.

Some of the men are silent, absorbing his latest bulletin to discuss later in private clusters with the old hands who have been here the longest and know how things work.

'It's simple mathematics,' Idris continues. 'You can work it out for yourself. Double the number of detectors means double the chances of getting caught, and double the time you'll be stuck here praying tonight's your lucky night.'

Nobody asks where he gets his information about the

inner workings of the port controls. They hear the logic, but they have to take him on trust.

'Of course there's always another way,' Idris says, rubbing his ruby ring as if for luck. A small crowd has coalesced around him. 'There's always the guaranteed option. It just depends on how long you're willing to wait.'

Aryan has been in the port long enough to know what that means; he has always dismissed it out of hand.

But men, stressed by repeated failure, by the debts they owe or their families owe or by their families' need for help, are starting to listen.

Aryan wills his feet to walk, but inertia anchors him to the spot.

'How cold would it get?' asks a man with sunken cheeks and hollow eyes.

'Yes, how long would we have to stay inside?' says another, his head so thin under its knitted hat that it looks like it's been squeezed between two doors.

Solemn faces crowd around. All of them are tired, cold to the sinews, exhausted in their minds. Idris sees he has their attention, and spools out his information in languid loops. This time, Aryan can tell, there are men among them who are ready to consider it.

'If you pick the right one, and that's why you need me, you can be standing under Big Ben in seven hours,' Idris says.

Seven hours. The number travels swift as rumour around the circle; the men repeat it under their breath. It seems unreal to them that they could be extricated from this quagmire in so little time, that in so few hours they could pass like ghosts through the walls of glass against which all their hopes have collided until now.

'Yes but how cold is it inside?' insists the man with the hollow face.

Idris fixes him with a look. Aryan can just make out the movement of his eyes behind the cold reflective glass.

'Minus 18, minus 20 at most,' Idris says. 'You take a couple of blankets with you and you'll be fine. Eskimos up in the Arctic live in minus 35 Celsius all winter long.'

Still, there is a murmuring. Seven hours in that sort of cold – you'd want to be sure you could get out when you'd had enough.

'If we get stuck inside, how long have we got?'

'Yes, how do we know we won't end up in an English supermarket – up there on a shelf with the frozen dinners?'

The men laugh. But something darker hovers behind the levity.

'Look, the ferry crossing takes ninety minutes at the most. Add on a couple of hours for customs at each end,' Idris says. 'That's five and a half hours. It's another hour to get to London – or two if the traffic's bad.'

'But what if the truck isn't going to London?'

'Look, this is Europe, you know – you're not in Pakistan now. Truckers aren't allowed to drive for more than four and a half hours without a break. So if you think you might feel chilly you throw on a couple more sweaters. If you feel a bit cold after you get through Dover, just bang on the wall – I'm sure the driver will be all too happy to let you out.'

'How many can you take on one of those trucks?' someone asks.

'Maximum of six,' Idris says. 'It's travelling first class, remember. Any more and your body heat will thaw the chickens out, and the driver will get suspicious if he hears them squawking and laying eggs.'

The men see through Idris's jokes, but they laugh anyway, perhaps because they need to laugh, and for a moment the tension ebbs.

Hamid can't stand having wet feet. He has moved his blankets into their hut and Aryan is sitting beside him out of the drizzle, watching him roll up wads of newspaper and stuff them into his shoes. In the last of the daylight, Kabir has gone with Khaled to fill the water bottles for the morning.

'Do you ever think about what life will be like in England?' Hamid says. A loose-leafed ball of newsprint flowers gently in his hand.

'It's hard to imagine,' Aryan says, 'except that I think we will always feel safe. And it's a good country because people believe in things being fair – at least that's what the tailor who taught me English used to say.'

'All I know is that it's very clean,' Hamid says. 'My father once said you could walk around London for an entire day and not get any dust on your shoes.'

Aryan ponders the wonder of it. It is a long time since he has thought about Afghanistan's dust-choked streets.

'Maybe they will have special buses for driving us to school,' Aryan says. 'And they will teach us about computers and the latest things in science.'

'Kabir tells me he is going to be a musician,' says Hamid. 'Maybe he'll turn into a rock star and we'll get to see him on TV.'

Aryan laughs. He pictures his brother strutting around a stage beneath a star-shaped electric guitar.

'Do you ever think about your family, about what they are doing now?' Aryan says.

Hamid's eyes drop. Too late, Aryan recognizes he has crossed a line. Like a border without a signpost, the landscape looks the same; he only knows he has passed over it when he realizes the language has changed.

'There's not much of it left these days,' Hamid says.

Aryan swallows. Yet now he has blundered into it, into the private things that no one ever discussed on the road, he senses something in Hamid that wants to go ahead.

'You never told me what happened,' Aryan says.

Hamid's voice when it comes now is soft and low, as if he is opening a hidden cavern in his heart. He weaves pictures for Aryan: a family in a northern village in the mountains, a celebration, a cousin who is about to be wed. But then the colour drains out of his story. Men arrive at the front door after nightfall, black turbans turning the threshold dark.

'They were on the hunt for traitors,' Hamid says, 'and that meant anyone with a weapon in their home.'

Suddenly children, brothers and sisters and cousins were being herded into a single room while the men in the black turbans set to work.

Hamid's hands are working at the newspaper again, unconsciously rolling wads of it into tight, illegible balls.

He heard it all through the door: the crack of whips, voices pleading, the hammerbursts of automatic weapons. He remembers sitting silently, close to the other children, huddled on the floor in the dark. He remembers hugging his smallest sister tight enough to block out the noise.

'Even after it stopped, and we heard them take off in their Toyotas, we didn't dare leave the room,' he says. 'It was hunger that finally drove us outside.'

It was the same in all the houses. They had killed all the adults in the village, men and women alike, just going from door to door.

Hamid's eyes are shiny and his throat is tight. The entire newspaper is shredded now into an arsenal of tiny spheres.

After that he went with his oldest cousin to Pakistan, though on the road they kept meeting other Afghans that Pakistan was pushing back the other way. Eventually they made it to a refugee camp near Peshawar.

'Because I was small I couldn't do much, but I carried things, and I worked in a tea-house pouring tea,' Hamid says. For a time he had a job as a carpet weaver, until even that work disappeared.

'I still had to send money for my sisters,' he says. 'That's why I had to keep going.' He went to Iran where first he found work in a light-bulb factory, then carrying boxes in a brewery, then pouring concrete for builders. But when he was cheated of his pay, and beaten and robbed, he abandoned Iran for Turkey. In Istanbul he laboured in different jobs until he found a place in the workshop with Mohamed.

Outside the hut, the wet clouds roll in from the sea and obscure the damaged moon. Aryan shivers under his cape of smoky blankets.

'What will you do in England?' Aryan says after a while.

Hamid's answer comes swift as rocket-fire. 'I want to study astronomy,' he says.

Hamid never ceased to surprise Aryan. In his home village, the teacher had shown up for an hour each day before going to another job to earn a living. Yet now he was talking about galaxies and telescopes and planets.

'You should have seen all the shooting stars I saw in Greece,' Hamid is saying. 'When you look at a star you are really looking back into the past because the starlight had to leave millions of years ago to reach us. It left a long time before the Russians and the Taliban and the warlords and the Americans and all the killing at home. It left before the Persians and the Mongols and the Egyptians – maybe that light set off when there were still dinosaurs left on Earth.'

'So if you study the stars, it will be like travelling backwards in time,' Aryan says.

'I just think that if we knew more about the universe, if we could imagine ourselves in space, we would be high off the ground, away from all our troubles, and we could see all of life beneath us. It would make all the fighting seem small and unimportant and pointless, and maybe it would make people like peace more.'

Hamid is a bit crazy, Aryan thinks, but sometimes he has good thoughts.

'I wish there were a way to turn back time and bring back all the people who died,' Aryan says. 'Well not all of them, not the bad ones. Just some.'

Hamid pauses a moment before replying.

'You lost people in your family too, didn't you?' he says.

Aryan nods.

They sit in silence, listening to the wind and the low growl of the trucks on the road to the port, each cloaked in their separate memories like a blanket of sorrow they shared.

Some time later Kabir's face appears in the triangular doorway.

'What are these for?' he says.

'They're for keeping people's little brothers out of our palace,' says Hamid. He lobs a paper missile at Kabir's nose.

Outside, the sea wind is starting to pick up. They listen to it worrying the plastic walls of the hut and nagging at its perimeter of thorns. They hear it churning up the waves and sifting through the dunes and whipping the dead campfires into eddies of ash and grit. It swoops past the lighthouse, glances off the roof of the cabin, hurdles the town hall and barrels towards the railway line, swinging the electric cables like skipping ropes and spinning the sign above the sawmill like a fairground attraction on its nail. It prances along the rafters where the Nigerian girls huddle in their third-hand sleeping bags. It rocks the trucks where the hauliers lie snoring in their bunks. It rattles the police barracks' windows, pries at the roof-tiles on the ferry captains' houses, and bowls cacophonous beer cans past the doorsteps of the soup-kitchen volunteers.

It interferes with dreams and unpicks sleep and unravels the dark spooling of the night.

The tide is out as they walk along the beach, away from the port, under the bruising dawn. Shreds of sky lie like bandages on the corrugated sand. England has retreated so far behind its angry sea that Aryan wonders if it weren't just a trick of the imagination, as insubstantial as a slide-show projected on cloud.

'We can do exercises to build up our rowing muscles,' Kabir is saying. Aryan has to turn his head sideways to catch his words before they are snatched away by the breeze.

Kabir has thrown himself on to the sand, demonstrating push-ups with his chubby arms. When he stands up again there are circles of soft sugar on his knees.

Kabir has become possessed by the idea of a boat. Whenever they go to the beach he ducks up into the dunes, or between the beach huts beyond the groynes, scouting for a dinghy or some sort of craft they can paddle across the Channel to England. A kayak, he says, would do, or maybe they could balance on a windsurfer.

Once he yanked up a child's inflatable canoe from under the seaweed, a yellow triangle that turned into a salt-bleached ribbon of plastic with fading Disney characters on the side. It tore out of the sand like a zipper.

'Don't even think about it,' Aryan had said, laughing and frowning at the same time.

Now Kabir is standing between Aryan and the sea and the world is in motion behind him, dark clouds sliding over pitching waves.

'Have you got any idea how far it is, Muscleman?' Aryan says. 'It is more than thirty kilometres.'

'Yes, but we'd have Hamid.'

'It would still be thirty kilometres,' Aryan says into the wind. 'Ten kilometres each – and that's if we went in a straight line.'

The black ink still on his fingertips makes their whorls look like the tide-ripples in the sand. He thrusts his fists deep into his pockets; the stain is like the imprint of failure that not even the salt water will wash off.

He watches an eclipse of cargo ships as he tries to think what to do. He is still exhausted after their efforts one night – no, two nights – ago; it is hard to hold on to his thoughts; one slides behind the other and he loses the trail.

'While we are looking for a boat we can still give the

trucks a try,' Kabir is saying. 'I don't take up much room, and on a big one we could both fit on together. Khaled says all we need is a plank of wood.'

Aryan tries to focus on Kabir's words. He knows his brother was impressed by Hamid's story, that it's been playing on his mind, that he thinks they could go to England tucked behind the wheels of a semi-trailer.

'And where are we going to get a plank of wood?' Aryan says.

'I don't know,' Kabir says. 'Sometimes they wash up on the beach. Or maybe someone is building a house.'

'You know Idris doesn't like freelances. He'd ban us from the other trucks if he found out.'

'Idris doesn't have to know,' Kabir says. 'And if we made it, we wouldn't care.'

'It's too risky, Kabir. Even if we did get past the controls.' He thinks about the cold and the water on the road, stone chips flicking into their faces, hands slipping off the dirt-caked steel.

Still, he would have tried it on his own. And he knows Kabir is game. But he has talked to Hamid and taken the measure of the danger – even supposing they got past the detectors in the port. With a conviction that reaches into a part of him that lies beyond words, he also knows he could never live with himself if anything ever happened to Kabir.

They trail along the invisible line where the hard sand turns soft, scuffing at clumps of seawrack and the slimy ink of jellyfish with their shoes. Two sets of footprints follow them, one meandering, the other looping and zigzagging across the beach.

Kabir fills his pockets with exploding sea grapes to toss into the campfire at night.

Aryan hears voices, distinguishes words, tries to relax into the rhythm of the truck as it crawls through the harbour controls. His hands are cold, and the taste of fear is on his tongue. Through his feet, through his legs and up into his chest, he can feel the powerful mechanics moving, the pistons and gadgets working, carrying them towards customs, towards the ferry, towards England.

Hamid smiled encouragement when he saw the cargo inside. Tomatoes, hundreds and hundreds of tomatoes, tiny ones, yellow ones, and red ones as spherical as marbles, and ovals, the shape of pigeon hearts.

'We're in luck,' he had said, making an O with his mouth and posting a tomato inside.

Plants, he has instructed them – cut flowers, vegetables, fruit – exhale carbon dioxide in the dark. 'They disguise your breathing from the detectors,' he told them. 'It's like they are still alive.'

Wedged among the crates, Kabir is leaning against Aryan. He has acquired a knitted hat from one of the men, and Aryan can smell the dampness of the wool.

Aryan's fingers search again for the crinkle of plastic inside his pocket. In the hut's half-light they had practised, one at a time, learning to conquer panic. They had drawn the bags over their heads and around their throats so the air couldn't escape until even Kabir could hold his breath for as long as his English counting.

They have chosen the biggest bags they could find, but still Aryan dreads the moment. He loathes the membrane's whisper as it sucks into his nostrils, its close-up synthetic smell, the feeling of light-headedness as he inhales the diminishing air. And now that the moment is near he is afraid of his own reactions. He imagines ripping the clinging plastic from his face, gasping like a landed fish for breath. He pictures fine red needles spinning like the gauge of catastrophe, electronic numbers whirling, the high-pitched squeal of alarms. Hey hey hey it's a hit, boys, let's see who we've got inside this van! He imagines the fury of the men and his sense of shame at being the one who let the others down.

As it happened, it was not the carbon-dioxide sensors that caught them but some other detector that eavesdropped on their rapidly beating hearts.

'OUT-OUT-OUT-OUT!' The port police extract them from the freight truck one by one, shouting at them in French, whacking the truck's metal struts with their truncheons. The driver stands in the pooling light beside the cabin, handing over papers to the guards. On the far side of the parking bay, three hyperactive sniffer dogs inspect a line of vehicles waiting their turn to board.

The air is chill and heavy with exhaust. They stand passively in the artificial light as the guards kick their feet apart and push their faces into the truck's grimy wall. One after another they are searched, bodies swept, mobile phones collected like a bucket of eggs.

It is routine for everyone: routine for the customs officers; routine for the guards; routine for the border police.

'Hello, you again!' one of them says to an Iraqi who has been halted there so often that he knows him by sight. 'Try again tomorrow, mate. Better luck next time.'

The Iraqi blinks back his humiliation in silence.

Glass doors slide shut on gliding runners. An officer working at a computer scarcely glances at them as they pass. He has straw-coloured hair and pinkish skin and a white crown embroidered on his shoulder.

The first English person Aryan has ever seen.

The back of the police van is cold and smells of metal. The floor is ribbed with dirt. Someone has painted the windows black so they can't see anything outside.

Shoeless, handcuffed, they sit hunched on two facing benches: a group of Afghans, one thin Iraqi, two young men from Iran.

Hamid is gazing at the floor. Kabir's pupils widen in the darkness.

The van rolls towards the exit, then abruptly stops. There is no way of telling whether they are inside or outside the port.

The double doors suddenly swing outwards. Three men built like bison crowd into the shrinking space. Bald heads. Army boots. No uniforms. Behind them, Aryan has the impression of darkness and a side of a fence.

When the Iraqi looks up they decide on him.

They can hear what is happening outside, even if they cannot see. There are no words. Just hard scuffling on gravel. The sound of blows. The van swaying as it is hit by something soft, then something hard. Strange, inchoate noises, like the moans of a dog.

Kabir's eyes are round with terror. Aryan wishes his hands were free to cover his ears.

When they bring him back the Iraqi lies, still hand-cuffed, on the floor of the van. He is curled up like a foetus. One eye is swollen shut and there is blood in his hair.

Kabir is crying. Aryan is shaking all over. He feels nauseous and stares at his knees.

Later, in the entrance to the detention centre, they sit for hours on a long, narrow seat. There is a window with nothing to look at but a car park and an outside wall.

The Iraqi is taken to a separate room. One foot drags on the floor as they hustle him by. 'Troublemaker,' one of the policemen says to the officer on duty as they pass.

Aryan's feet are wet and cold from walking across the gravel from the van. There is newsprint on the soles of Hamid's socks.

They wait their turn to stand before a policewoman. At

daybreak she takes their details. Name. Nationality. Age.

She indicates an electronic device with a small glass square on the top. She wears a machine-made sweater over her uniform. There is nothing personal about her, or the office, or the building. No decoration bar a portrait of a man in a sash on the wall. No photographs. Not even a plant.

'First your thumb,' she tells Aryan. 'Like this.' Her voice is neutral; she is just doing a job.

But something blocks. The machine refuses to work.

The policewoman abandons her attempts to fix it. Sliding an inkpad towards him, she points to where he has to leave his mark.

When he hesitates, she grasps his thumb and rolls it, once, from right to left and plants it on the white paper. Then the other fingers, one by one.

He feels exposed somehow, that something private about him is now in the light.

He stares at the black swirls. They look as fragile as seashells on the page.

It is mid-morning when they are finally let out. They collect their phones from an empty tabletop. Their shoes are lying in the drizzle outside.

But there are no shoes for one of the Iranians, and two of the Afghans find their pairs missing too.

The policewoman stares at them blankly when they ask.

They stumble into the street, hungry, cranky with lack of sleep. Aryan wonders which way to go. They are on the top of a hill, in a sort of industrial complex that is closed up and deserted for the weekend.

The drizzle has stopped but the clouds are violet and so heavy that they touch the earth. Their eyes stream in the cold; Aryan senses snow.

Hamid points out the lighthouse in the distance. 'That way's the sea,' he says. 'That way the port.' He has a sense of direction by now. He has been here before, seven times.

He sets off up the road, then stops and turns.

'You coming?' he says. 'Since they've brought us this far, we may as well take a look for ourselves.'

The tunnel hovers in their imaginations like some mythical, open-mawed beast. Down its throat, a day's march through the darkness; how simple it would be. One foot after the other, wind-rush locomotives screeching past them under the waves. Aryan pictures them hopping along the sleepers, or pressing themselves against walls slimy with seawater as carriages full of passengers flash by. There'd be English people drinking coffee, and French people reading magazines, or working on their computers, or chatting on their mobile phones; not even the driver would notice as they ducked along the rails. They wouldn't worry about the tankers and the ferries and the weight of water above them, nor even about the fissures where the sea was leaking in. Their faces would be turned to the distance, their fingers curled around an invisible thread, while always, calling them in and guiding them and shimmering like a lantern, the smallest circle of light that was England.

They cross wheat fields hacked to stubble for the winter, and clumps of grass turned to old-man's hair by the frost, then find themselves on a back road. A signpost announces Sangatte; another, Coquelles.

'The old roads always lead you somewhere,' Hamid is saying. 'It's the motorways that go right past the places you want to go.'

Hamid isn't sure exactly where it is, but he says they will hit the railway line if they can manage to steer parallel to the coast.

Aryan finds it hard to believe the sea is somewhere beyond the next rise. He imagines this shelterless landscape, exposed like naked skin to the lashing sky, stretching on for ever, crossed only by endless freeways and the single-file stride of power lines humming with electricity overhead.

A knot of trees clings to the horizon, their branches meshed and scratching at the sky. Perhaps there was once a forest here, and this is all that is left.

Kabir, who has run ahead, falls back in step with them. The cuffs of his trousers are already wet and one of his laces is undone. Aryan can tell he's been thinking.

'Hamid,' Kabir says.

'Yes, Kabir.'

'Why did the police keep those guys' shoes?'

'To make it hard for them to walk back,' Hamid says.

'But why would they make it hard for them to walk back?'

'So they will go away.'

Kabir ponders Hamid's answer for a moment. 'How can they go away if they don't have any shoes?'

Hamid's laugh has a hardness to it that Aryan doesn't recognize from before. 'That's one you'll have to put to the police,' he says.

They walk one behind the other along the gravel shoulder in case any cars come past.

'Hamid?'

'Yes, Kabir.'

'What's going to happen to that Iraqi man?'

Hamid shoots Aryan a sidelong glance.

'I don't know,' Hamid says.

The road flanks a hill that they decide to climb, hoping it will afford them a view. Their shoes glisten with water as they cut through the grass towards a hedge that is the same shape as the wind.

On the other side, graves line up as strict as hospital beds.

Kabir wanders over to a patch of gravel, then calls them over to see. A small group of headstones, inscribed with Arabic words.

'It's not that long ago,' Hamid says, reading the dates.

'I wonder who they were,' says Aryan.

A wreath of plastic flowers trembles in the cold.

Nearby they come across a tap. Aryan bends down to it, then makes Kabir drink as well. 'You won't feel so empty that way,' Aryan says.

He pictures the water curling its tentacles towards his belly.

Hamid beckons from the far side of the hilltop. A thread of silver carriages slips past, then disappears into the weft and warp of the land.

'It's got to be over there,' he says.

They gallop down the hillside and follow an old farm road that runs beneath the motorway; it peters out at a wider road that leads to a bridge.

Under it, rows of railway tracks stretch out like horizontal ladders. The three of them peer through the wire fence, staring at the small grey circle that must have swallowed up the train.

'There are two of them, two tunnels!' Kabir says. He gives a small hop of excitement.

As if he has sent the sky a signal, it starts to snow.

The twin entrances sit side by side, each bracketed by a safety exit bored above them into the hillside, ordinary, anticlimactic, as out of reach as the stars.

To Aryan, they look too small to be the gateway to

England. He had expected something grander: triumphal arches maybe, and decorations, and lights.

'You sure that's it?' he says.

'You think they put all these fences up for a rabbit hole under a hill?' says Hamid.

Through the twirling snow they can see access roads, and floodlights, and security cameras perched like hooded birds on the tops of poles. And multiple layers of fencing, even there on the bridge. And everywhere, razor wire, rolled into invisible blankets atop the walls of no-man's-land for as far as the eye can see.

'Are there landmines here too?' Kabir is saying.

'Not that I've heard,' says Hamid. 'But they've probably electrified the fence.'

Snowflakes settle on to their heads. Kabir squirms as Aryan dusts them off his hair and pulls the hood of his anorak over his ears.

'Where's your hat?' Aryan says.

Kabir pats his head, then pulls at his pockets. He turns up a striped plastic bag, a sea grape, and the blue plastic soldier he thought he had lost on the beach.

'Maybe it fell off in the truck,' he says.

A freight train shoots past them towards the tunnel; the latticed sides of its carriages turn the trucks into grimy mosaics. From a distance the wagons fill the entire entrance; Aryan can't see any space to walk alongside. And as the train goes in it neither stops nor decelerates enough for anyone to jump on board.

'It doesn't look too promising,' Hamid says.

Aryan turns the other way and peers down the vanishing rails. 'Do you think these fences go all the way back to Paris?' he says.

'Even if we could get around them, the cameras would still spot us along the tracks,' says Hamid.

'What about the safety exits?'

Hamid cocks his head, considering them. 'It's the same problem, don't you think?'

'We could jump off the bridge on to the top of a train,' says Kabir.

'Sure thing, Spiderman,' says Aryan. 'What about the rest of us?'

Hamid gives Kabir a friendly punch. 'There has got to be some other way,' he says.

Aryan's stomach growls. Now that they have seen the tunnel he is hollow with disappointment; it laces the cold around them with bitterness. He hadn't realized how much he had been counting on it; it was a fallback; it was a last-ditch reservoir of hope. But here, confronted by the sight and shape and sense of it, by the coils of wire and the electric fence and the dull-eyed stare of the cameras in the spiralling snow, he can feel its possibilities slipping through his fingers like a rope.

Fat snowflakes cloak the metal railings in fur. They gather in the angles of the razor wire, settle on the tops of the security cameras, and eddy like fainting butterflies on to the sleepers and the listening rails. They decorate the headstones in the graveyard, and rub out the footprints on the beaches, and fill in the exposed creases in the aching, hard-scrabble hills.

They ice up the decks of the ferryboats, and melt into the waves, and drape the south of England in the same billowing canopy of white.

Aryan buries his hands with their blackened fingertips deep inside his pockets. It seems to him that Calais is a city without doors.

It is dark by the time they get back to the lighthouse and the sky has exhausted itself. The snow that has finally stopped falling is freezing into a crust on the mud and the grass.

Men stand shivering and blowing on their hands and dancing like grim-faced boxers on the balls of their feet. The food line has already formed, though it is too early for the charity workers' van; the Kurdish youth on crutches is leaning against the wall.

The three of them have not eaten since the night before and Aryan is nearly fainting with hunger.

'Kabir! Where have you been?'

'Yes, where did you disappear to? We thought you were scooting around London on a big red bus!'

The older Afghans are gathering around his brother, forgetting the cold, laughing and chucking him under the chin. One of them produces a square of salvaged chocolate; another, a rusty toy car he'd found on the beach.

Kabir is grinning his big-toothed grin as the men tease him and shadowbox with him and muss up his overgrown hair.

'We went to see the tunnel,' Kabir says.

Aryan watches, and feels a stab that both engulfs him and makes him ashamed. It was the same twisting feeling he had in the workshop in Istanbul, when the other Afghans made a fuss of Kabir and clowned around with him and tried out their magic tricks.

He knows without ever discussing it that they all have people they have lost. He knows they have all left families behind, that they all have siblings or children they've not seen in months. He sees how their eyes light up and their faces relax whenever Kabir is around. He knows they would do anything to ensure he was safe from harm.

But sometimes, just sometimes, he wishes he could be the one they were glad to see. He wishes that someone would make a fuss over him, that someone would think he was special, that there were someone to watch over him.

Perhaps he is not fit for such a journey, he thinks. Perhaps he lacks the toughness of mind. Perhaps he lacks the resilience of which Hamid seemed to be made.

But then Kabir disarms him with his giggle, or baffles him with his questions, or produces more of his suggestions, and Aryan remembers they are all each other has, that they are a sort of team, and that together they will see the journey through.

On the way back to their shelter Khaled takes Aryan aside. 'You weren't seriously thinking about the tunnel?' he says.

'We just went to have a look. Since we were already near.'

'They say there's a graveyard somewhere around here where they buried the last guys who thought that was a good idea,' Khaled says.

Aryan stretches the ache from his limbs. He has slept badly despite his exhaustion, waking many times with the cold and the slats of the crate carving into his ribs.

They are standing round the campfire in the morning, boiling water for tea. Someone throws a plastic bottle into the flames and Aryan's eyes sting with the smoke.

Kabir has already given the canary water and poked a crust of bread through the wire cage, still trying to bribe or coax it into song. They have been to the beach with Khaled and dragged driftwood for the fire up through the dunes.

Hamid emerges, cursing, through the thorn bushes, four empty plastic bottles in his hands.

'They've cut off the water,' he says.

There is only one tap, some distance off, on the way to the Tioxide plant. Khaled has heard of another, so they set off to look.

They twist the tap in vain. It complains as it relinquishes a single, rusty tear.

At the cabin the charity workers are ladling out soup.

There are three hundred hungry men and the lowering cloud seems only to aggravate their mood. The air is frigid, and everyone seems irritable, agitated. There is shouting and shoving as the French people struggle to keep order in the lines. The Kurds are muttering at the Iraqis; Pashtuns and Hazaras are glaring their mutual mistrust; a Sudanese man said to be unbalanced is trying to push his way in.

'What's going on?' Aryan says to an Afghan ahead of him in the queue.

'Didn't you hear?' the man says. 'There's been a raid on the camp down by the canal. The police destroyed the shelters and arrested six guys and kicked their daypacks into the water. They lost their money, their papers, all their things.'

A group of Eritreans arrive behind them, out of breath. The police gave them the chase as they crossed the park on their way from the African squat.

'I thought there was meant to be a truce where they hand out the meals,' Khaled says in English.

'That doesn't stop them going for you on the way,' one of the Eritreans says. 'This morning they broke up one of the shelters in town. They've boarded it up with nails.'

Hamid looks at Aryan.

'Did you leave anything in the camp?'

'Only bedding,' Aryan says.

When they get back, the huts are all smashed up. Their blankets are trampled in the dirt. There are tracks in the mud where their firewood has been dragged away. The birdcage is lying on its side in the filth.

Kabir stands it upright. The door is open. A moment later he finds the canary cowering beside a rusting tin.

'You OK?' he asks.

The bird drags one flared wing behind it as it tries to hop away. Kabir scoops it up in his hands and blows gently to warm its feathers and places it back inside the cage.

Above them, the purple clouds hurt too much to snow.

At nightfall they trudge back towards the town, Aryan, Kabir, Hamid, plus Khaled and two of his friends who used to share his hut. Over their shoulders they carry the blankets they tried to dry over the bushes, heavy now with wetness and mud.

Through the fence they can see the trucks aligned in the waiting bays of the port, the white buildings, the cold bright lights coming on. Aryan tries to work out how far they'd got before the guards discovered them in the truck, where it was that the police van stopped and the men came to get the Iraqi man.

There aren't any warm air vents like there were in the pavements in Paris. So they look for a niche under a bridge, or under the back wall of a factory, or the ledge of a motor-way roundabout. Each time, they find that other people have already staked out a claim.

Finally they reach the goods entrance of a supermarket. The six of them roll the metal garbage skips across it to make a cave, but the howling wind bores straight at them between the wheels. With cold-stiffened hands they try to block the worst of it with packaging they salvage from inside.

'Aryan.'

Aryan isn't sleeping either. He is frightened he won't wake up if he closes his eyes.

'Aryan. It's too cold.'

Kabir is shuddering with it. Aryan can hardly feel his own hands and feet.

'Come on,' Aryan says. 'Let's keep moving.'

Hamid slides the skips apart. They set off, three slight shadows walking, walking, on the move all night through the silent streets.

Aryan has sworn to himself that they will try anything but the ice trucks. But now, his spirits ebbing on this hostile stretch of coast in the bleak midwinter, his mind keeps slithering back to Idris's words.

Seven hours.

He is starting to wonder if it isn't their best chance.

The long weeks of stasis are starting to gnaw at him. With every day that passes, with every night that finds them still in the streets, or slowly rebuilding their huts in the thorn bushes littered with refuse, Aryan feels his control over their lives slipping away. He is tired, tired, tired; the climate is wearing on him; every morning he is surprised he is still alive. Afghanistan was bitter in the winter, but he has never known cold like this – the way the wet air stings his eyes like needles, the way the wind off the sea bores through to his neck, to the small of his back, makes chilblains of his unwashed hands. The way its rimy fingers thumb through five layers of clothes.

Under numb feet, the puddles crack and splinter but do not melt.

Aryan tries to remember the last time he felt happy, and decides it is when they were on the move – in the back of a truck, in the train through Italy, in the carriage with the Americans-from-Iran. Every bump in the road, every flash of scenery made him feel they were getting closer to their goal. Where on the journey was it that they had stopped fleeing and started running towards a future, no matter how indistinct? Yet all that time, they were only getting closer to a wall. The harder he runs up against it, the more he feels his courage fray.

He tries to hide his despair from Kabir. It is not just the sense of being trapped. It is not just how hard it is to hold on to their hopes. It is something giving way inside.

There are moments when he feels like he is fragmenting. His memories are becoming disconnected slivers of time with gaps in the logic that links them. He remembers the coldest night, when the snow set to ice and a vengeful wind swept in from the north and the lights of the trucks were the only things creeping through the port. He remembers the old French people coming out of the blizzard to find them and take them to sleep on mattresses on the floor of a hall. But there are also empty expanses where he can't remember how they filled their days.

Sometimes he wonders if, in the unspoken things between them, Kabir can sense how he feels. Though sometimes he weighs upon him like the Earth itself, at others Aryan wonders who was sustaining whom, and whether, without his brother, he would have made it this far at all.

'I'm sorry, Kabir,' he says. The hand holding his plastic fork is raw and trembling with the cold.

Puzzled, his brother looks up from his tray of spaghetti. The road is black with water; they are sheltering from the sleet on the leeward side of a warehouse with their hand-out meal. The top of the lighthouse is invisible in the cloud, as if it has given up on ships and is looking out for aircraft instead.

'I'm sorry for bringing you here,' Aryan says. 'I should never have let you come. I should have gone by myself and sent for you from England. Maybe you could have flown all the way in a plane.'

'I wanted to come with you, Aryan,' Kabir says. 'I would have run away if you had made me stay in Iran. You're the only real family I have left.'

It is so long since they'd lived as a family that the word

comes as a shock to Aryan; he can hardly remember the time before everything imploded. For a moment it seems that his brother is referring to somebody else's life.

He looks at Kabir, at the overgrown hair, at the rain-slicked jacket over layers of clothes that have buried the Spiderman T-shirt he was once so excited to wear. He has changed, Aryan realizes. He is more serious than the Kabir he remembers with the puppies playing with his shoelaces in the onion fields. His puffy cheeks have thinned, and there are shadows around his eyes like he had when he was sick in Greece. If this journey is wearing him down, Aryan thinks, it is also taking its toll on Kabir; yet he never questions it, never says he wants to go back like he did when they arrived on the farm, never complains any more that he is nearly nine and still hasn't been to school. He never imagines there is any path other than the one they are on.

Aryan is anxious about time sliding by, that every day he is getting older and they might not let him into school, about how he should make a life. But Kabir accepts their situation with a sort of stoicism. His brother might have grown quieter, but for the first time Aryan notices how much he has come to rely on having him at his side.

Something moves inside Aryan, and he smiles. 'Remind me where we're going, Soldierboy,' he says.

'We're going to school!' comes Kabir's reply.

'And when are we going to get there?'

'At half past nine!'

'When?'

'On time!'

'And *how* are we going to get there?'

'KabulTehranIstanbulAthensRomeParisLondon!' says Kabir.

'Nearly there,' Aryan says. 'But I bet you I'll get there first.'

With his ruby-ringed hand Idris pulls a mobile phone and a wad of notes out of a bomber jacket that did not spend the night in the dunes.

'Look, if you're worried, I can get you to talk to someone who's made it across that way,' he tells Aryan. Idris is impatient, feigning fatigue. 'It's easy. We can ring them in England. Plenty of guys have done it. They go back and forwards whenever they like.'

'Let me think about it,' Aryan says. He does not trust Idris, but right now all he can see is a circle of diminishing options.

He wants to talk first with Hamid.

Khaled sells them a card for Aryan's phone. He got it for them at a supermarket on the edge of the town. Aryan doesn't ask how much he paid; he knows that the price already includes Khaled's commission.

They look for Jonah in the meal line, and find him sharing a cigarette on the African side of the cabin, beside the musical car.

'Still here, my friend!' Jonah says when he sees them, his

tired face made young again by his grin. He slaps his palm against Aryan's. His hair has grown springier since the night they spent in the rafters beside the sawmill; raindrops nestle in it like diamonds that match the one in his ear.

'You too,' Aryan says with a smile over the booming music. Faces lean out to see who Jonah is talking to, then pull back inside the car like a tortoise with multiple heads. The vehicle rocks to a reggae beat.

'I need your help again,' Aryan says. 'It's for the phone.'

'You need to charge it up?'

Aryan nods. He has long since lost his charger but he remembers that the Africans were pirating current for their batteries from a building site next to the sawmill. 'Would someone have a charger that fits?'

The phone gleams iridescent as a beetle on Aryan's proffered hand.

'No problemo, my friend,' Jonah says. 'We can do it this afternoon.'

'Do you want to talk to Masood if there's any time left at the end?' Aryan asks.

'Sure,' says Kabir. 'I'll tell him about the sea, and that we saw England from the beach.'

Aryan dials the number of the house in Tehran. There is an echo-filled pause like air rushing down a wind tunnel. There are strange click-clack sounds as the small current of hope races back across all the miles they have traced on foot, by boat, in the back of trucks and semi-trailers, on suspension-shot buses and trains. He imagines the signal beaming up to satellites and bouncing down to the cables that criss-crossed the city, snaking its way to the right street, the right pole, the right house, to the black Bakelite telephone, click-clack, click-clack in the silence as the call patches through.

He tries to guess who will pick up the receiver; his heart is bound tight with anticipation, joy chasing loneliness chasing anxiety chasing sadness at how long it has been. He pictures ruddy-faced Masood, and his sister Zohra who was teaching Masood to read, and their father Mustapha who scares Aryan a bit. He holds his breath; the line rings and rings into the void.

He counts nineteen rings before it cuts off.

'Wrong number,' he tells Kabir. His brother is waiting at his elbow, scuffing the ground with his heel.

He tries again.

He can see the phone in the hallway, just outside the living room they also used for eating and sleeping. He can remember the sound it makes which is different from the one carrying now down the crackly line.

He lets it ring until the line goes dead.

Something isn't right. Phone calls are so rare that there is always someone who will leap to pick up the receiver, or at least take a message for the family if no one is in.

He turns off the phone to save the battery and zips it back into his anorak, its hard shell close to his agitated heart.

In the evening they try again.

Aryan counts fourteen rings. Suddenly, a man's voice.

'Mustapha?' Aryan says.

'Who is this?' Aryan doesn't recognize the speaker.

'Aryan, the nephew of Mustapha,' he says. 'When will he be back?'

'Mustapha's gone, the whole family's gone,' the voice says.

'Gone where?' Aryan tries to make sense of the words.

'No idea where. Just gone. All the Afghans have gone.'

Aryan tries to grasp the news, to think fast as he absorbs the facts. Why would they have gone? Where would they have gone to?

'Who is speaking, please?' he says.

'I am Izad, the cousin of the owner of this house. My cousin has moved back to the city and needs his apartment again.'

'When did they leave?' Aryan's voice constricts. He tries to keep the man talking while he gropes for the right questions to ask, as the last thread connecting him and Kabir with the remnants of their family stretches as thin as the voice undulating feebly down the line.

'Last week,' says the man. 'I'm only here because Mustapha is coming back tonight to pay us the last month's rent.'

So they are still in Tehran. Aryan tries to think through the buzzing in his ears.

'I need to speak to him,' says Aryan. 'What time will he be there? I can call again.'

'He said he was coming tonight. Call back in an hour,' the voice says.

'Can you tell him Aryan called from France?'

But the receiver is already clattering in his ear. With the pip-pip-pip of broken connections something gives way in his chest.

Numb, he slides the phone shut. He shivers on the gritty black asphalt, gripped again by confusion. Tears needle the back of his eyes. He looks for somewhere private to go, but all he can see is the blurred blue light of a police car.

'What happened?' Kabir says. 'I thought you were going to let me talk to Masood.'

When they call again it is hailing. White stones bounce on the roadway, collect in the mud, turn the blankets that make up the sagging roofs of the huts into nests of crystalline eggs. Aryan's shoulder muscles hurt from always being hunched against the cold; his hands are so stiff he can hardly press the keys.

This time, Mustapha comes to the phone.

'We need money,' Aryan tells him. 'The agent here wants two thousand dollars. It's the only way to get across.'

Mustapha yells down the line. He has troubles of his own. He doesn't have that kind of money. While he and Kabir swan around Europe they have just lost their apartment and have moved in on top of another family who occupy a single room. There are more Iraqis moving into Iran, and there is no more room for long-term Afghan refugees.

Aryan doesn't try to explain. 'What are we going to do?' he asks.

Mustapha relents. 'I will ask around. Your father was well loved. Maybe there is something we can do.'

Two weeks later, Mustapha calls. He has the money; a middleman is holding it in trust. Aryan reads Idris's number down the phone so Mustapha can pass it on.

Aryan allows himself to think about his father properly for the first time in many months. Wonders about the families so grateful to him for teaching their children, even after he lost his job at the school, that they would agree to assist his orphaned sons. Marvels that he can still help them, though he died so long ago and is buried six thousand kilometres away.

Aryan saves Mustapha's mobile number in his phone, adding it to the three he has already stored in its memory: for Hamid, Idris, and the tailor's nephew in London.

Inside it doesn't seem so cold.

The carcasses swinging in two long lines don't look as sinister as he had thought. They are just sides of beef, Aryan tells himself, long dead, just chunks of meat destined for the dinner tables of England. They don't even have any heads.

There are six of them and they have climbed in at a petrol station on the edge of town. Idris has set it up and, after what they have been through in the previous weeks,

Aryan is surprised how smoothly it has gone. He is anxious about getting through the port, but Idris has said it will be a breeze, that they never check these vehicles because most people didn't like the cold. '*Bon voyage*,' he'd said as they'd shaken on the deal.

No, it doesn't seem so cold inside, not after the weather in Calais. There is a stillness, and Aryan realizes that for once, it's the lack of wind. In the darkness, under his blanket, he can feel Kabir sitting close beside him, knees to his chest, facing Hamid against the opposite wall. Three other men Aryan doesn't know are dispersed inside. They are wearing every item of clothing they could find – six sweaters each, two anoraks, and as many socks as they could manage and still fit into their shoes.

Idris's information is good; the truck gets under way soon after they clamber in.

Aryan has never been anywhere so dark. It's like the world before creation, before any memory of light.

The hands of Hamid's watch glow greenly: five forty-five am.

'How will we know when we're through the controls?' A voice is whispering in the blackness.

'We'll only be sure once we're on the ferry. The truck will park and stay still for a while, but we will feel the swell of the sea.'

'I hope it's calm. I don't want to get seasick.'

'Seasick – now you tell me,' comes the low reply.

They talk in soft voices, then fall silent. They are taking

enough risks as it is. Either they will get through or they'll be found; they are resigned; there is nothing more to do but hope.

They hear the truck rumble towards the ferry. It stops and starts and reverses. The hooks with their red and pink carcasses swing and squeak over their heads. There is a grinding of what sounds like metal, and then the truck stands still. The men's ears strain for the sound of voices, the sound of dogs, trying to imagine where they are in the port they have scoured endlessly from the other side of the wire.

The adrenalin that kept him warm is ebbing, and Aryan is starting to feel the cold of the metal seep through his clothes. He wraps the blanket around him, tight as a bandage. He has started to shiver, but can't bind the shivering down.

At first his mind races. It darts forward and back, rabbiting between anticipation and fear, digging out random moments from the places in which he had imagined a future. He remembers Bashir and Ali, the way he used to trail around with the brothers who are scarcely even memories now. It seems incomprehensible to him that they are not waiting for them to return to Afghanistan, that Bashir and probably Ali too are no longer alive. He reaches further back. He pushes away the horrible time with his cousin on the shores of the lake, before the soldiers came, and thinks instead about the chess games with Baba in the bazaar, about the way he got the old television to work with the car battery and the jump leads with their crocodile jaws. Then the picture surges up of what had happened to his body, gathering him up among the scattered apples, the wrenching sound of his mother's wails when they buried his remains at dusk.

Aryan forces himself to think about the house, the day his mother served the pomegranate seeds, the feel of the pigeons' soft white feathers and the scratching of their prehistoric feet on the roof, the stifling summer nights under the stars.

He remembers the house in Iran where he and Kabir and their mother lived with Zohra and Masood, and the bus back to Afghanistan, and the last time he saw Madar, the last sight of her sensible shoes. Her fatal choice to go just that day at just that time, just when the car bomber struck. All the events that that decision unleashed. He thinks back over his and Kabir's flight, the long journey back to Iran, the last moments at their cousin's house, the Kurdish smugglers in the mountains who were as frightening as the soldiers on the border. In Istanbul, the mechanical whirr of the sewing machines and the smell of cotton dust and the day he sewed up his hand. He remembers the night river crossing with Hamid, and the old woman's kitchen on the farm, and the puppies learning to dig, and Kabir's face in the dashboard light when the lorry driver brought him back to the farm.

He wonders how Solomon used the fares he robbed from them in Genova, and how the lady with the pram got by after Kabir stole her handbag in Rome. He remembers the touch of the woman's hands as she cut his hair. He thinks of the girl on the train, and her peacock eyelids in the reflection of the window at night. The Americans-from-Iran will be back in California by now, he thinks. He was happy the day they took them to buy new clothes.

It's getting cold, he says to Kabir, but his brother is lost in his own world.

Gradually Aryan's thoughts become heavy. It takes all his energy now to concentrate on not succumbing to the temperature, on gripping his jaws to stop the incessant chattering of his teeth. He covers his nose with his sweater to breathe his body heat back into his chest.

He is tired, so tired. It is so much effort to keep warm.

In his mind's eye Aryan sees the pigeons again. They are circling the city, white feathers flashing against the dark mountains, against the smoke of the chimneys, against the pastel washing on the lines. They are descending in slow revolutions, lower and lower, until he can feel the wind from their feathers brushing his face, and then the feathers themselves. He can't see his grandfather or hear his grandfather's voice but he knows he is somewhere near as the feathers caress his cheeks, and the birds' small hearts pulse warmly next to his skin. He is not afraid any more of their claws or the beating wings. Still they descend, so many of them they block out the sky and the houses and the wind. There is no place left to roost so they settle on his limbs and his body and his face, gently now, not scratching at all.

He can smell their feather scent, like dust and insects and seeds and the mountain wind, as they warm him like a coverlet, pressing down on him, closing in over his eyes and mouth and nose, smothering him with their softness and using up all the air.

Hamid and I were the only ones to walk out alive.

I don't know how long we waited in the end. Even Hamid was unconscious when they opened the truck. What saved us, I think, was that he and I were sitting near the doors; a thin trickle of air must have managed to filter in, and find its way to our noses and into our lungs, and kept up our low, slow breathing despite ourselves.

The first thing I remember of England was the market stench – rotting cabbage leaves and hosed-down meat – like a forest floor, like a field of compost – invading the metallic vacuum of cold.

A man in overalls was standing in the open doorway. His overalls were blue, the same colour as the sofa where the Queen was sitting in the photo with the dogs that were allowed inside. We were in some sort of loading zone.

'OhChrist,' the man was saying. His voice kept getting louder. 'OhChrist, what's this in here? OhJesusChrist, they're blue. Call someone, call an ambulance, JesusChrist, just do as I say, it's 999, don't argue with me. Go!'

Hamid was stirring a little but Aryan was lying slumped over me and he was cold like ice. It wasn't the temperature, they said later, it was the lack of oxygen. I pushed him off and got on my knees beside him and nearly fell down under those hanging carcasses and then I started slapping him about the face.

AryanAryanAryan.

Hamid was coming round with the fresh air. He got up too, kind of dazed, kind of crazy, not coming out at first with coherent words.

Kabir he kept saying Kabir Kabir we've got to go just run.

I was trying to wake up Aryan. His lips were blue and his eyes were shut and I couldn't get them to open up again.

AryanAryanAryan.

Hamid was yelling now Kabir you've got to run, and he stood up trembling and swaying and jumped down from the truck on buckling legs and tried to pull me with him. But I had Aryan on my knees I wanted him to wake up I had to wake him up because otherwise he wouldn't know where he was. And Hamid pulled my arm and then he ran and I saw him running and then he came back he came running back Kabir Kabir he said you've got to go you've got to run and he turned in a big wide circle away from me then back to me with tears all over his face and then finally he just ran.

Aryan didn't wake up. When the ambulance came all screaming wailing sirens like there'd been a big explosion they put a plastic mask across his face and pumped air into him from big grey tanks and thumped him on the chest and pushed everyone away but I wouldn't leave I kept calling him AryanAryanAryan to wake him up Aryan we're here AryanAryanKabulTehranIstanbul AthensRomeParisLondonAryan we made it but he didn't stir he didn't move he just lay there thin and blue under the equipment and the swirling flashing lights. Then they went to put him inside the ambulance but I wouldn't let go I screamed and screamed and gripped him hard with both my hands till they let me stay beside him and we went with the siren blaring to all oblivion through the English streets.

A lady from the hospital brought his mobile phone and his wallet and his notebook to the place where I am staying with other boys from all countries including England itself. In the notebook there were the drawings that Rahim had done of the park in Paris and Aryan's sums for the cost of the trip and the sketches he did of me with the puppies in Greece, and the lines where he counted the days, and the strange faces in the golden mosque in Istanbul, and the Kurdish peasants we stayed with in the mountains. There were also some bits of poems, and a drawing he hadn't shown me of a girl on a train. I called Zohra in Tehran and she went silent on the phone and wept until the last money ran out. I had to wait till they gave us more pocket money and then I could call the tailor's nephew. He said he couldn't come to get me because he wasn't legal. But at least he knew where I was.

So I stayed in the home for boys and went to school

with them. At first I only knew the English words that Aryan taught me – ea-gle, shep-herd, snow – though they weren't very useful in London. But I remembered all the numbers up to twenty, and I liked geography because I had seen so many places on our travels, and I liked learning what the symbols meant on maps.

I found an old chessboard in a cupboard at the home for boys but nobody knew how to play.

I missed Aryan so much. Sometimes at night he would come to talk to me. He reminded me about the puppies and the canary that couldn't fly or sing and the pigeons on the rooftop in Afghanistan. He asked me if I'd chosen a birthday month and told me never to forget I was an Afghan, even if I didn't remember much about it. He told me to make my way and start a new life, that English people were good people and believed in human rights, and to make sure I worked hard in school now that I had finally got there because so many boys we had known would never have the chance. And I was able to listen to music because the other boys showed me how to put it on Aryan's phone. I haven't started to play an instrument yet, but there is a teacher at the school who says she can show me on a pipe that's called a recorder. Once I get good, then all I will need is to find some English people planning to get married.

Sometimes I have nightmares about the man in Greece. I imagine that he is coming to find me and take me away in his truck. And sometimes I wake myself up with my own yelling when I dream about the things that happened to Baba and Madar. The only thing left inside Aryan's wallet was the folded-over photograph of our family from before I was born. So I take it out and look at it, and it makes me feel sad but also calm. And sometimes, when it gets very cold, I get the shakes because it reminds me of the way Aryan died, and then I try to hold it in by holding my breath but I can't stop the tears from coming. If the canteen ladies notice they bring me a cuppatea to warm me up. And I practise my counting, because it's true what Aryan said, that you can't count and be sad or frightened both at the same time.

About a year after I got here Hamid managed to find where I was. By mistake he called Aryan's mobile phone one evening, because he still had Aryan's number recorded in his own, and when I answered he couldn't believe it was me. I told him where I was staying and he came to see me one Saturday in the morning before he started his work. He had found a job washing up in a restaurant and was making some money but the hours were hard and he didn't like it how his clothes got drenched and his hands went wrinkly inside the gloves and how much he stank all over by the end of the night. They let him sleep in a space out the back and he had no shower but at least he could use the sink in the toilets. He hoped to move to something else, maybe waiting on tables where sometimes the custom-ers left tips. He didn't try to go to school any more because there was too much trouble back home, and now he had to send money to save his sister. But he worried all the time about not having papers, and said that if the police caught him they would try to send him back.

The thing about not going to school was that he would never get to study astronomy. But he said he still looked at the stars even though there was so much light at night-time over the city, and it made him feel peaceful to imagine ancient times, when the starlight first set off on its journey to Earth.

ACKNOWLEDGEMENTS

Warmest thanks to Barbara Trapido, Alexandra Pringle, David Miller, Sarah-Jane Forder, Polly Clark, Mark Harrison, Ann Brothers, Caroline McLeod, Janet Chimonyo, John Follain, Rita Cristofari, Paul Myers, William Spindler, Matthew Saltmarsh, Sylvain Piron, John Paul Rofé and everyone at Bloomsbury. My articles for the *International Herald Tribune* familiarized me with some of the locations traversed by Aryan and Kabir; I am most grateful to the late David Rampe, and to Susan Meiselas at Magnum, for their support and encouragement. Simone Troller at Human Rights Watch generously shared her insights into the situation of unaccompanied Afghan children and other separated minors across Europe, while Jean-Michel Centres and Mahvash Grisoni broadened my understanding of the daily circumstances of these children's lives. To all three, my deepest thanks. I have also drawn in places on Wali Mohammadi's brave account of his odyssey in imagining Aryan and Kabir's. To Nadjib Sirat, who steered me straight on so many points of Afghan life, my heartfelt thanks. Above all, I am indebted to the numerous young Afghans who, courageously or urgently or shyly or gradually, shared their experiences with me. In memory of my father, this story is for them.

A NOTE ON THE AUTHOR

Caroline Brothers was born in Australia. She has
a PhD in history from University College London
and has worked as a foreign correspondent in
Europe and Latin America. She currently lives in
Paris where she writes for the *International Herald
Tribune* and the *New York Times*. She is the author
of *War and Photography* and also writes short
stories. *Hinterland* is her first novel.

A NOTE ON THE TYPE

The text of this book is set in Linotype Goudy
Old Style. It was designed by Frederic Goudy
(1865–1947), an American designer whose
types were very popular during his lifetime,
and particularly fashionable in the 1940s. He
was also a craftsman who cut the metal
patterns for his type designs, engraved matrices
and cast type.

The design for Goudy Old Style is based on
Goudy Roman, with which it shares a 'hand-
wrought' appearance and asymmetrical serifs,
but unlike Goudy Roman its capitals are
modelled on Renaissance lettering.